SELECTED
STORIES

KJELL ASKILDSEN

SELECTED STORIES

TRANSLATED BY SEÁN KINSELLA

DALKEY ARCHIVE PRESS
Champaign / London / Dublin

These stories were selected from the volumes originally published as *Ingenting for ingenting, Et stort øde landskap, Hundene i Tessaloniki,* and *Samlede noveller* by Forlaget Oktober A/S, Oslo in 1982, 1991, 1996, and 1999

Library of Congress Cataloging-in-Publication Data

Askildsen, Kjell, 1929-
    [Short stories Selections. English]
    Selected stories / Kjell Askildsen ; translated by Seán Kinsella.
       pages cm
    ISBN 978-1-62897-028-9 (alk. paper)
       1. Askildsen, Kjell--Translations into English. I. Kinsella, Seán, (Translator) II. Title.
    PT8950.A769A2 2014
    839.823'74--dc23

                         2013048424

Partially funded by the Illinois Arts Council, a state agency
and the University of Illinois at Urbana-Champaign

This translation has been published with the financial support
of NORLA (Norwegian Literature Abroad) Foundation

www.dalkeyarchive.com

Cover photograph: portrait of Kjell Askildsen by Finn Ståle Felberg, felberg.org
Cover: design and composition Mikhail Iliatov
Printed on permanent/durable acid-free paper

SELECTED STORIES

Martin Hansen's Outing

Walking back towards the house, late one Friday afternoon in early August, I'd suddenly felt tired, as if I'd been carrying something heavy, although all I had been doing was tying up raspberry canes. I got to the steps, sat down on the second-to-last one, and thought: there's no one at home anyway. A moment later I heard voices from the living room, and before I managed to get to my feet, my daughter, Mona, said: What are you doing sitting here? I stood up and said: I didn't think there was anyone at home. We just got in, she said. We? I said. Me and Vera, she said. Vera and I, I said. Vera and I, she said. I began walking up the steps. Where's mom? she asked. At Granddad's, I said. I walked past her and into the living room, and thought: or wherever else she might be. Mona said: Can Vera and I sit out in the garden? Of course, I said. She asked if they could have a Coke. Where is she? I asked. In the toilet, said Mona. I said they could each have a Coke. I went up to the stairs and into the bedroom. The double bed was made. I wasn't tired anymore. Vera, I thought, isn't she the one who's always staring at me? I went over to the open window, and I stood there as they walked across the lawn over to the garden table. I thought: she must be at least a couple of years older than Mona. After a while, I went into the study and got the binoculars. I looked at her very closely, for a long time. I didn't look at Mona. I thought: you look good. Then I went over and lay down on the bed. I closed my eyes and pictured myself taking her. It wasn't difficult.

A half hour later I was sitting in the living room with a cup of coffee and a glass of brandy, when I heard Eli coming in the front door. I got up so that she wouldn't see me sitting idly. I took an encyclopedia from the bookshelf and opened it at a random page. She came into the living room. There you are, I said. Oh, yes, she said, it's hard to get away from him, I'm all he has. I don't think he's got too long left. I sat down. Is Mona not at home? she said. She's out in the garden, I said, with a friend. Has he gotten worse? Eli went over to the window. I don't know if I like Mona spending so much time with that Vera one, she said. Oh? I said. She's a lot older than her, almost sixteen, she should have friends her own age. I didn't answer; for a moment I wasn't sure if I'd removed the binoculars from the bedroom, and it made me feel slightly anxious. I asked her if she wanted me to make her a cup of coffee, but she had had at least three cups at the nursing home, she could, however, do with a glass of brandy. While I was getting it, I told her that my brother had phoned, that there was something he needed to talk to me about. Is that why you're drinking brandy? she said. I didn't reply. She sat down on the sofa. I handed her the glass. Is he coming here? she said. No, of course not, I said, I'm going to meet him in town. I walked over to the window. I looked at Vera and Mona and said: The raspberries are almost ripe. Yes, she said. I've tied them up, I said. Have you watered them? she said. It only rained three days ago, I said. I heard her putting down the glass and getting to her feet. I turned, looked at my watch and said: Well, I'd better get a move on. Are you going to be late? She asked. I don't know, I said.

When I got into town I felt slightly at a loss. I rarely go out alone, and I don't have a local. After having pottered around aimlessly in the streets for a while, I bought a newspaper and went into the bar at the *Hotell Norge*. It was empty. I bought a beer and spread the paper out on the table in front of me. I tried to think up things my brother would have wanted to talk to me about, but couldn't come up with anything. I leafed through the paper while I thought: all you have to do is just let everything take its course, just refrain from trying to bring things to a halt.

I left the bar an hour later; I was slightly drunk and correspondingly buoyed. A train of thought led me to recall something my father used to say to me, when as a boy I wasn't allowed to do something and I said: I will; He said: Your will is in my trouser pocket. And for the first time I wondered what his trouser pocket had to do with anything.

While I walked along puzzling this peripheral problem—what my will was doing in my father's trouser pocket; did he have his will in there too?—I came to a part of town I rarely frequent, and when I caught sight of a pub called "Johnnie," I felt an impulse, probably the very intention of the name, and went in. The premises consisted of a bar and three or four small tables. All the tables were taken. I went over to the bar and ordered a whisky; I wanted to get out of there quickly. Ice? said the barman. Neat, I said. A man came over to the bar. He spoke to me, he said: Good to see you again. I looked at him. I thought I might have seen him before. Likewise, I said. So you recognize me? he said. Yes, I said. That was some night, eh? he said. Yes, I said. Do you live here? he asked. Here? I said. Yeah, here in town? You know I do, I said. No, I didn't know that, he said. No, maybe I never mentioned it, I said. I finished my drink. I'm sitting over there, he said, come on over and have a chat. I told him I had to be getting on, I was already late, I was on my way to meet my brother. That's a pity, he said. Some other time, I said. Yes, he said. Regards to Maria, that's her name, isn't it? That's right, I said. Then I left. I felt completely sober. I wondered if he'd ever meet whomever he thought he'd met.

I ended up roaming the streets; it was only half-past nine and I didn't feel like going home. Although, I didn't feel like doing anything else either. I walked over the bridge and all the way to the railway station. There were a number of people standing on the platform waiting for a southbound train. A voice came over the PA and announced the train would be eight minutes delayed. I went into the station restaurant, bought a beer at the bar and sat down at a table by the window. I managed to drain the glass before the train arrived. When the train left, I went to the toilet. There must have been someone standing in one of the cubicles waiting for a victim. I felt a blow against my head, and then nothing, before I came around, alone, on the floor. I threw up, and just then the door opened. I wanted to stand up. A voice cried something out. I think he thought I was drunk, and I wanted to say something, but

I wasn't able to. I don't remember everything very clearly. I didn't make any more attempts to get to my feet. After a little while I was picked up and helped out of the toilet and into an office. I was set down on a chair. I had vomit on my jacket. I was ashamed. I was driven to the hospital in an ambulance. A doctor shone a light into my eyes and ears and asked me a few questions, which I answered, and then he left. I lay there staring at the ceiling, and then he came back and asked how I felt. I told him my head hurt. I'd say it does, he said, you have a mild concussion. I asked if I could call home to get my wife to come and collect me. Just a moment, he said and disappeared again. I sat up. A nurse came in with my jacket and my shirt; I'd thrown up on them as well. We got most of it out, she said. Thank you, I said. There's a payphone out in the hall on the right hand side, she said. I don't have any money, I said. No, of course not, she said. She left. I put on my shirt. She came back with a cordless phone, then she left me on my own. I tapped in the number. It took a long time for Eli to answer. It's me, I said, do you think you could come collect me, I'm at the hospital, at the A&E, it's nothing serious, but I've had my wallet stolen and I've—At the A&E? she said. Yes, I said. Oh Martin, she said. It's nothing serious, I said. I'm on my way, she said.

She came half an hour later. She was quite calm; she had that soft expression she sometimes has when she's asleep. She stroked my cheek. She said she had spoken to the doctor. I pulled on my jacket. She looked at it. I've thrown up, I said. I know, she said. We walked through the corridor and the waiting room and out to the car. Wasn't William with you? She said. No, I said, I was alone. She didn't say any more. My head was pounding. I've been on my own all night, I said. She didn't answer. We drove over the bridge and past *Hotell Norge*. Didn't he show up? she asked. He didn't call, I said. After a while I turned and looked at her; she pretended not to notice. When we were almost home, she said: Are you taking advantage of the situation to tell me something you otherwise wouldn't have been able to bring yourself to say? I'm just telling it like it is, I said. Yes, okay, she said, but why? What's the point of all this sudden honesty? I didn't reply. She drove in the gate and pulled up in front of the garage. I got out of the car and walked to the front door. I unlocked it and went inside. I poured myself a glass of brandy and knocked it back. What are you doing? she said from behind me. My head is sore, I said. The doctor said you weren't to drink alcohol, she said. Come to bed instead. I didn't know what to do. Then I realized that it didn't matter what I did. Okay, I said.

I'd been lying there a while when she came into the bedroom. She turned off the light before getting undressed, either because she saw I was awake, or in spite of it. She didn't say anything before getting into bed, then she said: I've told Mona you were going to meet William. Presumably you don't have any objections to saying he didn't show up? I didn't reply. Have you? she said. No, I said. Good night, she said. Good night, I said.

It took me a while to fall asleep. I thought about what she'd said: What's the point of all this sudden honesty? Then I thought: what does she know about me that I don't know that she knows?

When I awoke, she was already up. I tried to go back asleep. My head was sore. It was past nine. I had to go to the toilet, and I made as little noise as possible so that she wouldn't hear me. I didn't flush. I went back to bed, but couldn't sleep. I got up, parted the curtains slightly and saw Eli and Mona sitting at the garden table, eating breakfast. I dressed quickly and went down to them. Mona wanted to know everything. Eli went to fetch me a cup of tea. Mona couldn't understand why I'd been at the restaurant at the railway station. I explained it to her. So it was actually Uncle William's fault, she said. It wasn't as if I needed to go there just because he didn't turn up, I said. No, but still, she said. I didn't reply. She continued quizzing me. Eli came back with the tea; she sat down. Did the ambulance have its siren on? asked Mona. I don't think so, I said. But the lights were flashing? she said. Let your father eat now, said Eli. I don't know, I said. We sat in silence for a while. Then Mona mentioned that she had to do something before she went to the beach, and Eli asked whom she was going with. Vera, said Mona, and I waited for Eli to say something about that, but she didn't. Who's Vera? I said. You know who she is, said Mona, the one who was here yesterday. Oh right, I said. Eli didn't say anything. Mona stood up and left. Now it's our turn, I thought, but Eli just asked how I felt. I replied that I was fine, apart from having a slightly sore head. Good, she said. She got up and began to clear the table; she only had enough room on the tray for half of the things. I watched her as she walked across the lawn, I thought: she hasn't even asked me how much there was in my wallet. Then I remembered how she'd stroked me across the cheek, and when she came back I wanted to say something, but she beat me to it. She asked if I'd told Mona that William hadn't shown up. Yes, I said, and she thought it was his fault things turned out the way they did. So what? she said. No, nothing, I said. No, because it couldn't possibly bother you, she said, after all it's quite natural for one lie to lead to another. It's not the way you think, I said. What do you know about what I think? she said. Tell me what you think I think. I didn't reply. She cleared the rest of the table with jerky movements then she said: Tell me, was it in a moment of weakness or of strength that you came clean about William? I didn't reply. She left. I thought: fuck her.

After a while I stood up and walked past the raspberries over to the only spot in the garden where you can't be seen from the house. I hadn't found the answer to that last question she'd asked me. I sat down on the stump of the big, diseased birch tree that we'd felled four years ago; I sat facing the cypress hedge that backed onto the side road; through one of the gaps in the hedge, I could see the broken fence-pale which Eli still hadn't noticed, and which I still hadn't got around to replacing, and suddenly it struck me that my non-disclosure and falsehoods were prerequisites for my freedom, and that my admission in the car had been an expression of indifference arising from the situation, which had nothing to do with honesty.

Rather elated at having clarified this, I got up and went back to the garden table. The veranda door was open. I intended to tell her that I was sorry for having said it wasn't true that I had arranged to meet William. Just then she came out onto the veranda. I'm off to visit Dad, she called, and then went back inside.

I sat there until I was sure she had left, and then went in, closed the veranda door, locked it, and went up to the bedroom. I kicked off my sandals and lay down. I thought about her having said: Oh Martin, and that she had stroked my cheek. After a while I slipped into a doze filled with images: changing landscapes I had not seen before, and of which there was nothing frightening, but which nevertheless filled me with such a strong feeling of unease or anxiety that I had to get out of bed and pace back and forth on the bedroom floor. It helped. It's always helped. But I didn't lie down again.

A little while after Eli got home—we hadn't spoken to one another, she was standing by the kitchen window looking out—I went over to her, laid my hand gently upon her and told her I was sorry for having said that I was going to meet William. Yes, well, she said. I withdrew my hand. It didn't have anything to do with you, I said. Oh Martin, she said. I didn't know what else to say, but I didn't leave. She turned and looked at me. I met her gaze. I couldn't make out what was in it. This doesn't change anything, she said. No, I thought. Does it? she said. No, I said.

The Dogs of Thessaloniki

We drank morning coffee in the garden. We hardly spoke. Beate got up and put the cups on the tray. We should probably take the chairs up onto the veranda, she said. Why? I said. It looks like rain, she said. Rain? I said, there's not a cloud in the sky. There's a nip in the air, she said, don't you think? No, I said. Maybe I'm mistaken, she said. She walked up the steps onto the veranda and into the living room. I sat there for another quarter of an hour, and then carried one of the chairs up to the veranda. I stood a while looking at the woods on the other side of the fence, but there was nothing to see. I could hear the sound of Beate humming coming from the open door. She must have heard the weather forecast of course, I thought. I went back down into the garden and walked around to the front of the house, over to the mailbox beside the black wrought-iron gate. It was empty. I closed the gate, which for some reason or another had been open; then I noticed someone had thrown up just outside it. I became annoyed. I attached the garden hose to the water tap by the cellar door and turned the water on full, and then dragged the hose after me over to the gate. The jet of water hit at slightly the wrong angle, and some of the vomit spattered into the garden, the rest spread out over the asphalt. There were no drains nearby, so all I succeeded in doing was moving the yellowish substance four or five meters away from the gate. But even so, it was a relief to get a bit of distance from the filthy mess.

When I'd turned off the water tap and coiled up the hose, I didn't know what to do. I went up to the veranda and sat down. After a few minutes I heard Beate begin to hum again; it sounded as though she was thinking about something she liked thinking about, she probably thought I couldn't hear her. I coughed, and it went quiet. She came out and said: I didn't know you were sitting here. She had put on makeup. Are you going somewhere? I said. No, she said. I turned my face toward the garden and said: Some idiot's thrown up just outside the gate. Oh? she said. A proper mess, I said. She didn't reply. I stood up. Do you have a cigarette? she said. I gave her one, and a light. Thanks, she said. I walked down from the veranda and sat at the garden table. Beate stood on the veranda smoking. She threw the half-finished cigarette down onto the gravel at the bottom of the steps. What's the point of that? I said. It'll burn up, she said. She went into the living room. I stared at the thin band of smoke rising almost straight up from the cigarette, I didn't want it to burn up. After a little while I stood up, I felt unsettled. I walked down to the gate in the wooden fence, crossed the narrow patch of meadow and went into the woods. I stopped just inside the edge of the woods and sat down on a stump, almost concealed behind some scrub. Beate came out onto the veranda. She looked towards where I was sitting and called my name. She can't see me, I thought. She walked down into the garden and around the house. She walked back up onto the veranda again. Once again she looked towards where I was sitting. She couldn't possibly see me, I thought. She turned and went into the living room.

When we were sitting at the dinner table, Beate said: There he is again. Who? I said. The man, she said, at the edge of the woods, just by the big . . . No, now he's gone again. I got up and went over to the window. Where? I said. By the big pine tree, she said. Are you sure it's the same man? I said. I think so, she said. There's nobody there now, I said. No, he's gone, she said. I went back to the table. I said: Surely you couldn't possibly make out if it was the same man from that distance. Beate didn't reply right away, then she said: I would have recognized you. That's different, I said. You know me. We ate in silence for a while. Then she said: By the way, why didn't you answer me when I called you? Called me? I said. I saw you, she said. Then why did you walk all the way around the house? I said. So you wouldn't realize I'd seen you, she said. I didn't think you saw me, I said. Why didn't you answer? she said. It wasn't really necessary to answer when I didn't think you'd seen me, I said. After all I could have been somewhere else entirely. If you hadn't seen me, and if you hadn't pretended as if you hadn't seen me, then this wouldn't have been a problem. Dear, she said, it really isn't a problem.

We didn't say anything else for a while. Beate kept turning her head and looking out of the window. I said: It didn't rain. No, she said, it's holding off. I put down my knife and fork, leaned back in the chair and said: You know, sometimes you annoy me. Oh, she said. You can never admit that you're wrong, I said. But of course I can, she said. I'm often wrong. Everybody is. Absolutely everybody. I just looked at her, and I could see that she knew she'd gone too far. She stood up. She took hold of the gravy boat and the empty vegetable plate and went into the kitchen. She didn't come back in. I stood up too. I put on my jacket, then stood for a while, listening, but it was completely quiet. I went out into the garden, around to the front of the house and out onto the road. I walked east, away from town. I was annoyed. The villa gardens on both sides of the road lay empty, and I didn't hear any sounds other than the steady drone from the motorway. I left the houses behind me and walked out onto the large plain that stretches all the way to the fjord.

I got to the fjord close to a little outdoor café and I sat down at a table right by the water. I bought a glass of beer and lit a cigarette. I was hot, but didn't remove my jacket as I presumed I had patches of sweat under the arms of my shirt. I was sitting with all the customers in the café behind me; I had the fjord and the distant, wooded hillsides in front of me. The murmur of hushed conversation and the gentle gurgle of the water between the rocks by the shore put me in a drowsy, absentminded state. My thoughts pursued seemingly illogical courses, which were not unpleasant, on the contrary I had an extraordinary feeling of wellbeing, which made it all the more incomprehensible that, without any noticeable transition, I became gripped by a feeling of anxious desertion. There was something complete about both the angst and the desertion that, in a way, suspended time, but it probably didn't take more than a few seconds before my senses steered me back to the present.

I walked home the same way I had come, across the large plain.

The sun was nearing the mountains in the west; a haze lingered over the town, and there wasn't the slightest nip in the air. I noticed I was reluctant to go home, and suddenly I thought, and it was a distinct thought: if only she were dead.

But I continued on home. I walked through the gate and around the side of the house. Beate was sitting at the garden table; her older brother was sitting opposite her. I went over to them, I felt completely relaxed. We exchanged a few insignificant words. Beate didn't ask where I had been, and neither of them encouraged me to join them, something that, with a plausible excuse, I would have declined anyway.

I went up to the bedroom, hung up my jacket, and took off my shirt. Beate's side of the double bed wasn't made. There was an ashtray on the nightstand with two butts in it, and beside the ashtray lay an open book, face down. I closed the book; I brought the ashtray into the bathroom and flushed the butts down the toilet. Then I undressed and turned on the shower, but the water was only lukewarm, almost cold, and my shower turned out to be quite different and a good deal shorter than I'd imagined.

While I stood by the open bedroom window getting dressed, I heard Beate laugh. I quickly finished and went down into the laundry room in the basement; I could observe her through the window there without being seen. She was sitting back in the chair, with her dress hiked far up on her parted thighs and her hands clasped behind her neck making the thin material of the dress tight across her breasts. There was something indecent about the posture that excited me, and my excitement was only heightened by the fact she was sitting like that in full view of a man, albeit her brother.

I stood looking at her for a while; she wasn't sitting more than seven or eight meters away from me, but because of the perennials in the flowerbed right outside the basement window, I was sure that she wouldn't notice me. I tried to make out what they were saying, but they spoke in low tones, conspicuously low tones, I thought. Then she stood up, as did her brother, and I hurried up the basement stairs and into the kitchen. I turned on the cold-water tap and fetched a glass, but she didn't come in, so I turned off the water tap and put the glass back.

When I'd calmed down, I went into the living room and sat down to leaf through an engineering periodical. The sun had gone down, but it wasn't necessary to turn the lights on as yet. I leafed back and forth through the pages. The veranda door was open. I lit a cigarette. I heard the distant sound of an airplane, otherwise it was completely quiet. I grew restless again, and I got to my feet and went out into the garden. There was nobody there. The gate in the wooden fence was ajar. I walked over and closed it. I thought: she's probably looking at me from behind the scrub. I walked back to the garden table, moved one of the chairs slightly so that the back of it faced the woods, and sat down. I convinced myself that I wouldn't have noticed it if there had been someone standing in the laundry room looking at me. I smoked two cigarettes. It was beginning to get dark, but the air was still and mild, almost warm. A pale crescent moon lay over the hill to the east, and the time was a little after ten o'clock. I smoked another cigarette. Then I heard a faint creak from the gate, but I didn't turn around. She sat down and placed a little bouquet of wildflowers on the garden table. What a lovely evening, she said. Yes, I said. Do you have a cigarette? she said. I gave her one, and a light. Then, in that eager, childlike voice I've always found hard to resist, she said: I'll fetch a bottle of wine, shall I?—and before I'd decided what answer to give, she stood up, took hold of the bouquet and hurried across the lawn and up the steps of the veranda. I thought: now she's going to act as if nothing has happened. Then I thought: then again, nothing has happened. Nothing she knows about. And when she came with the wine, two glasses and even a blue check tablecloth, I was almost completely calm. She had switched the light on above the veranda door, and I turned my chair so I was sitting facing the woods. Beate filled the glasses, and we drank. Mmm, she said, lovely. The woods lay like a black silhouette against the pale blue sky. It's so quiet, she said. Yes, I said.

I held out the cigarette pack to her, but she didn't want one. I took one myself. Look at the new moon, she said. Yes, I said. It's so thin, she said. I sipped my wine. In the Mediterranean it's on its side, she said. I didn't reply. Do you remember the dogs in Thessaloniki that got stuck together after they'd mated, she said. In Kavala, I said. All the old men outside the café shouting and screaming, she said, and the dogs howling and struggling to get free from one another. And when we got out of the town, there was a thin new moon like that on its side, and we wanted each other, do you remember? Yes, I said. Beate poured more wine into the glasses. Then we sat in silence, for a while, for quite a while. Her words had made me uneasy, and the subsequent silence only heightened my unease. I searched for something to say, something diversionary and everyday. Beate got to her feet. She came around the garden table and stopped behind me. I grew afraid, I thought: now she's going to do something to me. And when I felt her hands on my neck, I gave a start, and jumped forward in the chair. At almost the very same moment I realized what I had done and without turning around, I said: You scared me. She didn't answer. I leaned back in the chair. I could hear her breathing. Then she left.

Finally I stood up to go inside. It had grown completely dark. I had drunk up the wine and thought up what I was going to say, it had taken some time. I brought the glasses and the empty bottle but, after having thought about it, left the blue check tablecloth where it was. The living room was empty. I went into the kitchen and placed the bottle and the glasses beside the sink. It was a little past eleven o'clock. I locked the veranda door and switched off the lights, and then I walked upstairs to the bedroom. The bedside light was on. Beate was lying with her face turned away and was asleep, or pretending to be. My duvet was pulled back, and on the sheet lay the cane I'd used after my accident the year we'd got married. I picked it up and was about to put it under the bed, but then changed my mind. I stood with it in my hand while staring at the curve of her hips under the thin summer duvet and was almost overcome by sudden desire. Then I hurried out and went down to the living room. I had brought the walking stick with me, and without quite knowing why, I brought it down hard across my thigh, and broke it in two. My leg smarted from the blow, and I calmed down. I went into the study and switched on the light above the drawing board. Then I turned it off and lay down on the sofa, pulled the blanket over me and closed my eyes. I could picture Beate clearly. I opened my eyes, but I could still see her.

I woke a few times during the night, and I got up early. I went into the living room to remove the cane, I didn't want Beate to see that I'd broken it. She was sitting on the sofa. She looked at me. Good morning, she said. I nodded. She continued to look at me. Have we fallen out? she said. No, I said. She kept her gaze fixed on me, I couldn't manage to read it. I sat down to get away from it. You misunderstood, I said. I didn't notice you getting up, I was lost in my own thoughts, and when I suddenly felt your hands on my neck, I mean, I see how it could make you ... but I didn't know you were standing there. She didn't say anything. I looked at her, met the same inscrutable gaze. You have to believe me, I said. She looked away. Yes, she said, I do, don't I.

Elisabeth

It was early Sunday morning. I had taken a deckchair from the veranda and carried it down to the corner of the garden, next to the flagpole, and was sitting there reading *The Anarchist*. My brother and his wife weren't up yet. I glanced up at the house now and again, at their bedroom window, but the blinds were down. I'd got to the part where Esch seduces Frau Hentjen, where she reluctantly lets go of the curtain, allowing him to force her into the dark alcove, and over to her conjugal bed, and I felt myself aroused by the rape-like scene. Just then Elisabeth, my sister-in-law, appeared in the open bedroom window, but I pretended not to see her.

A little while later she called me in for breakfast. There were only the two of us. She said David had a headache. She sat opposite me, and I took even more pleasure in looking at her now than I had the previous night, which may have been partially due to my still being in the grip of my earlier excitement. She sat looking at her plate for the most part, and the few times I made eye contact, she glanced quickly away. Mainly to keep an all too insistent silence at bay, I asked her the type of questions it was reasonable to ask a sister-in-law you've known for less than twenty-four hours, and she answered with striking eagerness, as if each new question was a lifeline to be clasped. But she still avoided my gaze, and with her eyes averted, mine were allowed free rein. And what I saw, led me to fantasize and picture things with obvious references to Frau Hentjen's reluctant submission in the dark alcove.

After breakfast I went across town to see my mother. My boy, she said, stroking my cheek. She had grown so old, there was hardly anything left of her. I walked ahead of her into the kitchen. I sat down at the table. Oh Frank, really, she said, we should sit in the living room. Can't we just sit here, I said. She made a pot of coffee and thanked me for the cards, especially the one from Jerusalem. You've been to Jerusalem, imagine that, she said. Did you visit Golgotha? No, I said, I didn't make it there. Ah, she said, that's a pity. Your father and I talked about it so often, about Jerusalem being the place we'd most like to visit, and Golgotha and Gethsemane were the two spots we'd most like to see. I didn't answer, but I smiled at her. She put two cups on the table and asked if I'd like a slice of cake. I told her I had just eaten breakfast. She glanced at the clock on the shelf beside the window, and then she asked me what I thought of Elisabeth. I said that I thought she was very nice. Do you think so? she said, well, I hope you're right. What do you mean? I asked. Oh, I don't know, she said, I don't think she's too good for Daniel. No one's good enough for Daniel, I said. Anyway, she said, let's not talk about it anymore. We didn't talk about it or anything else for a while. I hadn't seen her in two years; time and distance had made me repress my dislike of her; now it stirred. You haven't changed, she said. No, I answered, what's done is done.

I sat there for almost an hour; I did my best to avoid any topics that could emphasize the distance between us, and the visit could have petered out in a conciliatory atmosphere if she hadn't found it necessary to tell me how many times she'd prayed that I'd find my way back to Jesus. I listened to her awhile, then I said: Stop going on, Mother. I can't, she said, tears welling up in her eyes. I stood up. Then it's probably best I go, I said. You're very hard-hearted, she said. Me? I said. She walked me to the door. Thank you for the visit, she said. Goodbye, Mother, I said. Say hello to Daniel, she said. Not Elisabeth? I said. Of course, her too. God bless you, Son.

I went straight to the restaurant at the railway station and drank two pints. I calmed down somewhat. A train arrived from the south. It remained at the platform for a couple of minutes, and just before it began to move again, Daniel alighted from one of the carriages. With an intuitive feeling of having seen something I wasn't supposed to see, I quickly turned my head the other way. When I couldn't hear the train anymore, I looked out at the platform again. It was empty. I stayed sitting a little while longer, then I drank up and left.

When I got back to my brother's house, Daniel hadn't come home. I told Elisabeth that my mother said hello. Didn't you run into Daniel? she asked. No, I said. He went to meet you, she said. At Mother's? I said. Yes, she said.

I fetched *The Anarchist* from the living room and walked down to the end of the garden. The deckchair was in the sun, so I moved it beneath the shade of the apple tree. Elisabeth came out onto the veranda and asked if I'd like a cup of coffee, and a little while later she brought it down to me. She was slender and petite, and as she walked towards me across the lawn, I thought how easy it would be to lift her up. Thank you so much, Elisabeth, I said. She smiled and went straight back to the house, and I was left to contemplate the gap between a risqué thought and a concrete act.

Daniel came home half an hour later. He'd changed into shorts and a colorful shirt that was unbuttoned and thus displayed that hairy chest of his that I'd once envied him, long ago. He lay on his back in the grass and closed his eyes to the sun. We chatted about nothing in particular. At one point a woman opened a window in the house next door, and just after that she came out into the garden and sat down where I could see her. Daniel told me about a colleague of his, whom he claimed I knew, and who had recently died of bowel cancer. The woman in the garden next door went back into the house. I was bored. I said I had to go to the bathroom. I brought the empty coffee cup with me. Elisabeth wasn't in the living room or in the kitchen. I went up the stairs to my room. Through the window I could see that Daniel had got to his feet and was standing, looking through *The Anarchist*. Not really your kind of thing, I thought. The woman came out of the house next door; I could see her mouth moving, and Daniel went over to the fence. I flopped down on the bed, thinking that I shouldn't have come, that I should have remembered how little I had in common with Daniel. I only lay there for a few minutes, then I walked down the stairs and out into the garden. Daniel wasn't there. I leafed back through the book to read the scene between Esch and Frau Hentjen again, but just then Daniel came out of the neighbor's veranda door. He jumped over the fence. He looked in high spirits. I was just helping the neighbor move a cupboard, he said, and then he went over to the water tap by the cellar door and rinsed his hands. Do you want a beer? he called. Yes, please, I called. I put the book on the grass. He came back with two bottles of pilsner. Has Elisabeth gone out? I asked. She'll be back soon, he replied. He lay down on the grass and told me I shouldn't sit in the shade. I didn't reply. Ah, this is the life, he said. I didn't reply. Isn't it? he said. Sure is, I said. Elisabeth came from around the side of the house. I got to my feet. Take a seat, I said, and I'll fetch another chair. She said it was okay, she could get one herself. I went up to the veranda and brought back a folding chair. She hadn't sat down. Thank you, she said. My brother's a gentleman, said Daniel. Yes, she said. She sat so she could see both of us. I just want to make a good impression, I said. Did you hear that, Elisabeth? said Daniel. Yes, she said. When you were a kid, Daniel said, you used to always bring Mom home a bouquet of wildflowers, do you remember? I didn't remember. No, I said, I don't remember that. Do you not remember? Mom was always saying: that's my boy, and sometimes you got a slice of bread with sugar on top. Do you not remember me snatching it out of your hand once, and then stamping on it in the gravel at the bottom of the steps? No, I said, I don't remember that. I can't remember anything from when I was small. You must have been at least seven or eight, he said. I don't remember anything from when I was small either, said Elisabeth. Daniel laughed. What are you laughing at? asked Elisabeth. Nothing, he said. She bowed her head and looked down at her hands, I couldn't see her eyes. Then she threw her head back abruptly and stood up. Right, well, I'll just go and . . . she said. She left. I closed my eyes. Daniel didn't say anything. I thought about how he had altered something in the story about the slice of bread: He had eaten half of it, and I was the one who had knocked it out of his hand, making it land on the gravel. I opened my eyes and looked at him, and I felt a mild distaste at the sight of his hairy chest. He lay there smacking his thin lips, and then he said: What do you think of her? I like her, I said. He sat up and took a swig of the bottle, then leaned back and looked up at the sky, but he didn't say anything. I got to my feet and walked across the lawn, towards the little vegetable patch where lettuce, chives and a row of sugar snap peas were growing. I thought: how am I going to stick this for a week. I pinched a pea pod loose, and Daniel called: Elisabeth is toying with self-sufficiency. I ate the pod, then I walked back to Daniel and said: I've always wanted a vegetable garden with sugar snaps, turnips and radishes. In that case, he said, Elisabeth is just right for you. Don't you want her anymore? I asked. He looked at me. What's that supposed to mean? he said. It was a joke, I said. He stared at me and then he lay down and closed his eyes. I said I had a letter I needed to write, and I picked up my book and left. I met Elisabeth on the way upstairs. Your vegetable garden is lovely, I said. Oh, that, she said. I tasted a sugar snap, I said. She was standing one step above me and we were looking right at one another, and again I thought: she'd be easy to lift up. Just help yourself to them, she said. Thanks, I said. I looked away, and she continued on down the stairs. I should have held her gaze a little longer, I thought. I went up to my room and lay down on the bed.

I was awoken by a thunderclap. The sky was dark and I was cold. I got up and closed the window. Lightning split the sky, followed right after by a fierce downpour. It was nice to look at.

I went down to the living room. Daniel was standing by the veranda door. The storm had put me in a conciliatory frame of mind, and I went over to him and said: Isn't it spectacular? Spectacular? he said. The apple trees are being stripped of fruit, and look at the sugar snaps. I looked at them; some of the stalks lay on the ground. Yes, that's a pity, I said, but they can be tied up again. I don't think so, he said. Sure they can, I said, I'll do it.

After a while the storm passed, and the leaves and grass glistened in the sun. I asked David for some twine. You'll have to ask Elisabeth, he said. She was in the kitchen. She looked like she'd been crying. She gave me a ball of twine and a scissors. I went outside. There were four or five unripe apples lying under each of the three apple trees. I tied up the pea stalks, it didn't take long, and then I went up and sat down on the veranda. I didn't feel like going inside.

At dinner the tension between Daniel and Elisabeth was so acute that every attempt I made to get a conversation going fell flat on its face. In the end we sat there in silence. Something irresistible built and built within me, and before I'd finished eating, I put down my knife and fork, stood up and said: Thanks, that was lovely. I was aware of Daniel looking up, but I didn't want to make eye contact. I went up to my room and got my coat, and then I went out. I made my way through town to the restaurant at the railway station. I sat with a beer and a feeling of unease pounded away inside me. A man with a beer glass in his hand came over to the table and asked if he could sit down. I rebuffed him, but he still sat down. I stood up and went to find another table. He sat three tables away, staring at me. I pretended not to notice. I drained my glass and went to get another beer. When I returned, I sat down on the opposite side of the table, with my back to him. I thought about Daniel, how he had got off the train, how he had rinsed his hands after being at the neighbor's, and how he had laughed at Elisabeth. I thought about Elisabeth, too. Then my tormentor came and sat down opposite me. I'm not so easy to shake, he said. Get lost, I said. Tut-tut, he said. Get lost! I said. Tut-tut, tut-tut, he said. I got to my feet. I took the glass and threw its contents in his face. Then I turned to go. I walked quickly, but didn't look around before I'd reached the door. He wasn't coming after me, he was sitting, drying his face with the tablecloth.

I arrived home just as the sun was going down. I let myself in. The house was quiet. I walked into the living room. Daniel was sitting there. Well, well, he said, you're back. I didn't reply. Where've you been? he said. For a walk, I said. I sat down. You just up and left, he said. I didn't reply. He didn't say any more; he sat looking out of the window. Has Elisabeth gone out? I said. She's gone to bed, he said. He continued looking out of the window, and then he said: Might be for the best if you were on your way. The thought had occurred to me, I said. Not that I mind having you here, or anything, he said. No? He glanced at me, but didn't reply. I stood up. I went over to the table by the veranda door and fetched *The Anarchist.* It's Elisabeth, he said, she's not quite herself at the moment. Oh? I said. I don't really want to talk about it, he said. I walked towards the door. I'll leave tomorrow, I said. He said my name just as I was closing the door behind me, but I pretended not to hear. I went up the stairs and into my room. It was beginning to get dark, but I didn't turn on the light. I sat down by the window. Apart from the grasshoppers, everything was quiet. I wasn't tired, I felt much too cold inside. After a good while I heard footsteps on the stairs, and the sound of a door being opened. Then it went quiet again.

I undressed in the dark because I had an image of Elisabeth in my mind, which I was afraid wouldn't withstand the light. And perhaps I brought the image over into my sleep, because at some point during the night I was awoken by a dream about a woman lashed to the belly of a large animal.

In the morning it was raining, a quiet, steady downpour. I heard sounds from downstairs, and I didn't want to get up, I wanted to wait until Daniel and Elisabeth had gone to work. While I lay waiting, I fell asleep.

I woke up again around nine, and twenty minutes later I went down the stairs and into the living room. It wasn't raining any longer, and I wanted to go out into the garden, but the key to the veranda door was gone. I walked into the kitchen. The breakfast things were out and a place had been set for me, and beside the plate lay a sheet of paper. It read: Pity you have to leave. Elisabeth thinks so too. Hope it's nothing serious. Just leave the key under one of the seat cushions on the veranda. Thanks, Daniel.

I read it twice. Then I understood.

I put the sheet back exactly as I'd found it, then I went up to the first floor and into Elisabeth and Daniel's bedroom. I hadn't been in there before. The bed was made. I wasn't looking for anything in particular. There were no clothes over the backs of the chairs, and there was nothing on the nightstands to show who slept where. I opened the door to a closet where dresses and suits were hanging. I wasn't looking for anything in particular. I went out of the bedroom and into my room. I began packing my suitcase. It didn't take long. I carried it down to the hall. It was almost two hours until the train left. I sat down in the living room. I'd had a persistent thought in my head that had refused to budge since I'd read his note. I tore a page from the notebook and wrote: Such a pity about Elisabeth. Hope it's nothing serious. Give her my best. I'll leave the key in the post box. Frank.

The Grasshopper

Maria made a remark about him in front of the others, which he found inappropriate and that peeved him. He did his best to seem unperturbed, but when the guests had gone and Maria said she was tired, he opened another bottle of wine and put a log on the fire. Aren't you coming to bed? she said. He replied that he wasn't tired and he felt like another drink. She looked at him. Tomorrow's another day, she said. I'm aware of that, he said, and that was the only hint of aggression he managed to express.

He stayed up for an hour. He drank two glasses of wine. Then he took the bottle into the kitchen and emptied most of the wine into the sink. He brought the bottle back out and placed it beside the empty glass.

He woke up late the next day and he was alone in bed. He got up straight away. The house was empty, and the table was set for breakfast—but just for him. The coffee in the thermos was lukewarm. He drank two cups. The Sunday paper lay beside the plate. He picked it up and went out onto the veranda. Maria was on her knees in the vegetable garden, almost hidden behind the dahlias; he pretended he didn't see her and sat down with his back to her. He opened the paper and sat looking over the top of it: some treetops, a pale blue sky. He sat like that until he heard footsteps on the gravel and her voice behind him: Good morning. He lowered the paper and looked at her. Good morning, he said. She pulled off her gardening gloves and came up the steps. Did you stay up long? A couple of hours, he said. That long? she said. He folded the paper, without replying, and then he said: I was thinking about going to visit Dad. But I've invited Vera to lunch, she said. I'll be back by then, he said. You won't make it, she said. So we'll eat an hour later then, he said. Just because you suddenly decide that you want to visit your father? He didn't reply. She went inside. He got up and went in after her to get his coat. You haven't even eaten, she said. I'm not hungry, he said. He met her gaze; she studied him. What's the matter with you, she said. Nothing, he said.

Later on, as he was driving out of town in the direction of R, he felt almost cocky, and he thought: I do as I please.

Halfway to R he left the motorway and drove towards the end of the Bu fjord. There was a small outdoor café there, and he bought two sandwiches and a coffee. He sat under a tree and looked out over the fjord. He lit up a cigarette. Now and then he checked his watch. He smoked two more cigarettes, then he got to his feet and walked slowly back to the car.

He drove the same way back, and he arrived home before they'd sat down to eat. Maria asked how his father was, and he said: He didn't recognize me. Vera said that it must be difficult seeing your father so utterly helpless. He nodded. They sat down to eat. He poured them red wine. They ate roast beef. They talked about everyday things, he offered the odd yes and no in agreement; his thoughts were often elsewhere, but he made sure the whole time that the wine glasses were never empty. And when, towards the end of the meal, Maria wanted to hear more about his father's condition, her question collided with an aggressive thought he'd just had, and his reply was rather rash and dismissive: You're suddenly very interested in my father. There was utter silence. Then, in a low voice, Vera said: That wasn't a very nice thing to say, Jakob. No, he answered, almost as quietly, but it's got nothing to do with you. He took hold of his glass, his hand trembling. I think you ought to explain yourself, said Maria. He didn't reply. I don't know what to think, she said. He leaned back in the chair and looked at her. He said: Dad is fine. He doesn't know what's going on around him anymore, but if the nurses are kind to him, then he's in safe hands. So he's fine. It grew quiet again, then Maria said: You could have just said that straight off. There's a lot of things that could be said straight off, he said. What do you mean by that? she said. Do I mean something by it? he said. Really, she said, now you're just being impossible. She stood up and began clearing the table, and when Vera got up as well, she said: No, no, just sit down. Jakob saw Vera hesitate, then she picked up the vegetable bowl and the gravy boat and followed Maria into the kitchen. Jakob poured himself some wine, then he got to his feet, picked up his glass and went out onto the veranda. He smoked a cigarette, then he smoked one more. His glass was soon empty. Vera came out. She sat down. What a summer, she said. Yes, he said. But actually, she said, August is quite ... There's something wistful about it, don't you think, like it's the end of something. He looked at her, didn't reply. As a child, she said, I always associated August, especially the evenings, with grasshoppers, their song, I thought it was so nice. Now there are no grasshoppers anymore. Aren't there? he said. No, she said. He looked at her; she was sitting with her head lowered, examining a fingernail. He said: Would you like some wine? Yes, please, she said. He went in and fetched a bottle and a glass. Maria wasn't there. Vera was sitting in the same position, as though lost in thought, and when he had filled her glass, and his own, and was standing looking down at her for a moment, a sudden warmth passed through him, like a jolt, and he said: You look so pretty. Me? she said. He didn't reply, just sat down. It was completely quiet for a while. Then she said: It's a long time since anyone has said that. Can I have a cigarette? He held the pack out to her. I didn't know you smoked, he said. No, she said, I've quit. He gave her a light. From the doorway, Maria said: Oh Vera, really. I know, said Vera. Has Jakob led you astray? Vera looked at Jakob and said: Yes, in a way. But I made up my own mind to follow him. Maria came out onto the veranda, pulled a chair over to the table and sat down. Jakob asked if he should get her a glass, he felt light and free. He fetched the glass and poured some wine into it. Vera blew smoke rings. Look, she said, I can still do it. You're play-ing with fire, said Maria. Yes, said Vera, I'd almost forgotten how good it was. I told you, said Maria. Vera blew more rings up into the almost still air. You're putting your willpower to the test now, said Maria. Spare me, said Vera. She looked at Jakob, and added: Maria's never quite got over being the big sister. I can hear that, he said. Rubbish, said Maria. Maria doesn't play with fire, said Jakob. Oh, I'm sure she does, said Vera, isn't that right, Maria? Everyone does. Maria sipped at her glass. Could well be, she said, but I avoid getting burnt. Jakob laughed. Maria looked at him. Vera put out the cigarette. It's humid, said Maria. Yes, said Vera. Imagine if there were a real thunderstorm. And a bolt of lightning struck that ugly house over there. Oh Vera, really, said Maria. Jakob laughed. Did you think that was funny? said Maria. Yes, said Jakob, that's why I laughed. It was completely quiet, for a long time, then Maria got to her feet. She stood for a moment, then she walked to the steps and down into the garden. Say something, said Vera. He didn't reply. He poured wine into her glass. I'm getting tipsy, she said. And why not, he said, that's what wine's for. I think I'll be off, she said. I'd like it if you stayed, he said. I'll just turn naughty, she said. So do, he said. Naughty girl, she said, looking at him. He looked away, but could feel she was still looking at him. Are you getting nervous now? she said. Not nervous, he said. What then? she said. Maria came across the lawn. The carrots are bumping into one another, she said. Bumping? said Jakob. They need to be thinned, she said. She came up the steps and placed three small tomatoes on the table. Taste how good they are, she said. Vera picked one up. I think I'll find myself a man with a garden as well, she said. Yes, why not? said Maria. And a veranda like this, said Vera, where you can sit even when it's raining. We never sit here when it rains, said Maria. Of course we do, said Jakob. I often sit here when it rains. You do not, said Maria. I certainly do, said Jakob. I would have sat here in any case, said Vera. She put the tomato in her mouth. Along with my husband, she said. What husband? said Maria. The one with the garden and the veranda, said Vera. You're tipsy, said Maria. Yes, indeed, said Vera. I'll make some coffee, said Maria. She went inside. Vera took a large gulp of wine. Coffee! she said. Jakob filled up her glass. Thanks, she said. And a cigarette, if you have one. He gave her a cigarette, and a light. Is it true you sit here when it's raining? she said. On occasion, he said, but it's been a long time since I have. So it wasn't true then, she said. No, he said, but there was no way Maria could know that. But you made her out to be a liar, she said. No more than she made me out to be a liar by saying that I haven't sat here. But that's the truth, said

Vera. Yes, but she doesn't know that. Maybe she knows it because she knows you, said Vera. She doesn't know me, said Jakob. Maria came out and put down three cups. She looked at Vera, but didn't say anything. She went back inside. Poor Maria, said Vera. Jakob didn't reply. I'm going to have a coffee and then I'll be off, she said. He didn't reply. She put out the cigarette. Maria brought the coffee, poured it into the cups and sat down. Jakob got up and walked into the living room, down the hall, and out onto the street; he stood for a moment, then he set off towards the center of town.

He came home two hours later. Vera and Maria were sitting in the living room; they still hadn't switched on the lights. There you are, said Maria. Yes, he said. We were just sitting here wondering where you'd got to, said Maria. I had to buy cigarettes, he said. It was completely quiet for a while, then he said: It's getting cloudy. Yes, said Maria, we saw that. We heard a grasshopper, said Vera. Oh? said Jakob. He glanced at her; she looked away. He took the cigarette pack out of his pocket. Would you like one? he said. No thanks, said Vera, I've quit again. He lit one for himself. Anyone care for a beer? he said. They didn't. He went out to the kitchen and fetched a bottle, took a glass, came back, and sat down. Nobody spoke. Well, I'd better be off home, Vera said. You're welcome to stay the night, said Maria. I won't, but thanks, said Vera. After all, there's no one waiting for you, said Maria. No, come to think of it, there isn't, said Vera. I don't have anyone waiting up for me. You make it sound like you feel sorry for me. Nonsense, said Maria, nobody feels sorry for you, why would anyone feel sorry for you? No, that's what I'm saying, said Vera, so don't ask me to stay because there's no one waiting for me. I could just as well stay even if there was someone waiting for me. Yes, of course, said Maria. Vera got up. Are you going? said Maria. I'm going to the toilet, said Vera. Jakob followed her with his eyes. She's so difficult, said Maria. Jakob didn't reply. Maria stood up and turned on the floor lamp. And you just disappeared, she said. He didn't reply. She stood beside the light; he didn't look at her. He heard her breathing was fast and heavy, then she said. I can't take this much longer. Right, he said. Is that all you've got to say, she said. He didn't reply. Oh Christ, she said. Jakob heard Vera coming down the stairs. Maria turned off the lamp and sat down. The room was almost dark. Vera came into the living room, went over to the open veranda door, and stood looking out. Jakob got to his feet. I should be getting off before it starts to rain, said Vera. Jakob walked down the hall, and into the guestroom. He closed the door. The bed was made. He stood for a few seconds looking at it, and he felt a quiver run through him. Then he went to the window. The bank of cloud had drawn very close; it split the sky in two. He pulled a chair over. He sat with his elbows resting on the windowsill looking out at the dusk. After a while he heard low voices coming from the hall, then the door being opened, then it went quiet. He didn't move. Suddenly a wind swept through the leaves of the tree outside the window, and a few moments later the rain came. She didn't make it, he thought. He tried to detect sounds in the house, but heard only the rain. It had grown almost completely dark. And all at once it went bright, and a few seconds later distant thunder could be heard. Maria will be scared now, he thought. There was more lightning and more thunder; he counted the seconds; the intervals grew shorter and shorter. She's scared now, he thought. He got up and went to the door, opened it slightly and listened. He stood like that for a while, then he went down the hall into the living room. Maria wasn't there. He went back out and up the stairs, into the bedroom. She was lying with the duvet over her head. Maria, he said. She pulled the duvet aside. She was fully dressed. I was so scared, she said. There's nothing to be scared of, he said. I thought you'd left, she said. He went over to the window. Don't stand there, she said, please. He saw her reflection in the pane. It's not dangerous, he said, we have lightning rods. I know, she said, but it scares me, and it scares me even more when you stand there. He took a couple of steps back; he could still see her. She got out of bed. Looks like it's over now, he said. I thought you had gone, she said. Where would I have gone, he said.

A Lovely Spot

—Aren't you driving a little fast? she said.

—No, he said.

A little while later he turned off the motorway and onto the narrow, winding road towards the fjord.

—It's so green since we were last here.

—Yes, he said.

—It's as if the road is narrower, she said.

—I'm not driving too fast, he said.

Just before they got to the big oak tree where he usually left the car, she said she had a feeling that something wasn't quite right. She usually said that when they were drawing close to the summerhouse, and he didn't reply. One time she may be right, he thought.

He parked the car. He helped her with the lightest backpack.

—Just start walking, he said.

—I'll wait for you, she said.

—I'll catch up, he said.

He caught up with her halfway down the steep, overgrown dirt road. She was standing waiting for him.

—Is it heavy? he asked.

—No, she said.

They walked on. After a few minutes the house came into view below them. He slowed down; she always walked in front for the last few meters. She opened the gate, then she said:

—Somebody's been here.

—Oh? he said.

—I left a stone on the gatepost, she said, and now it's gone.

—Well, he said, I guess somebody's taken it. Was there something special about it?

—No, she said, an ordinary stone.

He closed the gate after himself.

—I don't like the fact someone's been here, she said. He didn't reply. He saw that the apple tree was in bloom.

—Look at the apple tree, he said.

—Yes, she said, isn't it beautiful.

She reached the door. She took off the backpack. He walked over to her, placed the shopping bags beside her backpack and took the key from his pocket.

—Do you want to open it? he asked.

—You do it, she said.

He opened the door and went inside. He put down his backpack on the kitchen floor and continued into the living room. He opened a window and stood looking out over the fjord. She called to him. He went out to her.

—Would you be a dear and hoist the flag, she said.

—Now? he said.

—I like people to see that we're here.

He looked at her, then picked up the shopping bags and went back inside. He fetched the flag from the drawer of the dresser in the hall.

—It was always the first thing Dad did, she said, hoist the flag.

—Yes, he said, I'm aware of that.

—You don't mind, do you?

—I just did it, didn't I! he said.

He went over to the flagpole.

They were by the kitchen table. They had eaten. She sat looking out of the window, in the direction of the dense forest.

—Isn't this a lovely spot, she said.

—Certainly is, he said.

—I don't think there's anyone who has a nicer place, she said.

He didn't reply.

—I just wish we could cut back all that scrub at the edge of the forest.

—Why? he said.

—It's just so . . . you can't see what's behind it.

—It's not on our property, he said.

—No, she said, but still. Dad used to always cut it back.

They sat in silence for a while.

—What will we do tomorrow? she said.

—Are we going to do something? he said.

—No, I don't know, she said. Take the rowboat out. To Ormøya, for example.

—It's nice just being here, he said.

—Of course. Yes, we'll stay put then, will we? Besides we've got plenty to do here.

—We're going to take it easy tomorrow, he said.

—But the outside toilet needs to be emptied, she said.

—There's no hurry, he said.

—No, just as long as it gets done.

They stood on the quay, the sun was about to set.

—Oh, how I love this place, she said.

He didn't say anything.

—There. I fell into the sea right there.

—Yes, he said, you've told me.

—I must have been about four years old, she said.

—Five, he said.

—Yes, maybe. I struck my head against one of the stones you can see there and it left a deep cut above my ear, and if Dad hadn't— what was that?

—It sounded like an animal, he said.

—It was someone shouting, she said.

—No, it sounded more like an animal.

—Let's go inside, she said.

They walked towards the house.

—We have to remember to take down the flag, she said.

—It's not necessary, he said.

—We've always done it, she said.

—Yes, he said, I know.

—There's a rule requiring you to, she said.

—I know, he said.

—I want you to do it, Martin. If not, I'll do it myself.

—All right, all right, I'll do it.

When he came in, he said:

—I'm opening a bottle of wine.

—Yes, do that, she said.

She sat down on the bench. He poured wine into her glass.

—Thanks, that's enough, she said.

He poured himself twice as much and sat down by the window.

—That's where Dad used to sit, she said.

—Yes, you've told me, he said. And where did your mother usually sit?

—Mom? She . . . Why do you ask?

—I was just wondering. Cheers.

—I think she normally sat here on the bench.

She sipped at her wine. They sat in silence. He pushed his chair back a little so he could look out at the fjord without having to turn his head. He drank.

—It's so quiet, she said.

He didn't reply. Then he said:

—There's a man standing over there on the headland.

She got up and went to the window.

—He's looking this way, she said.

She opened the window.

—Why are you opening the window? he said.

—So he'll see that there's somebody here.

—Why? he said.

—So he'll keep away. You see, now he's gone.

She closed the window and went and sat down.

He looked at her.

—Why are you looking at me like that? she said.

—I'm just looking at you, he said. Cheers.

He drained the glass, got up, went over to the table and poured more wine into it.

—Have you locked the door? she said.

—No, he said.

—Could you do it, she said.

—When we're going to bed, he said. We never lock it before we go to bed.

—Just this once, she said.

—Why?

She didn't reply. He went out into the hall. He opened the door and looked towards the gate and the forest, then he closed and locked it. He stood a few moments in the half-light of the hall, all he could hear was his own breath.

—Martin, she said.

He went in to her.

—I thought you'd gone out, she said.

He didn't reply. He took a gulp from his glass. She checked the time.

—I think I'll go to bed soon, she said.

—Yeah, do that, he said.

—Are you going to bed? she said.

—Not just yet. It's nice to sit and look out at the fjord.

—Yes, isn't it? she said. Isn't it a lovely spot?

—Certainly is, he said.

He looked at her.

—I think you're looking at me so strangely, she said.

—You think? he said.

She took hold of her glass. She drank up.

—I'm sorry I'm so tired, she said. It's probably all the fresh air.

—Yes, he said. Just go on to bed.

She was asleep. He undressed and crept under the duvet. She was lying with her back to him. After a while he placed his hand on her hip. She gave a low moan. He left his hand there. He felt his member grow. He moved his hand a little further down. Her body gave a start, as if from an electric shock. He withdrew his hand and turned the other way.

He had been up to the car and to fetch a coil of rope. On the way back he stopped by the gate and stood surveying the house and property. Then he picked up a stone and put it on the gatepost. He walked down around the front of the house and over to the boat-house. She was lying on the quay reading. He hung the rope on a peg under the eave, then he sat down with his back to the wall and looked out over the fjord.

After a few minutes he went over to her. She looked up and smiled.
　—Isn't it lovely? she said.
　—Isn't what lovely? he said.
　—Lovely here, she said.
　—Certainly is, he said.
　—Why don't you fetch the other mattress and lie down here in the sun, she said.
　He didn't reply. He looked up at the house and said:
　—The swallows haven't arrived yet.
　—They could be here any time, she said. It's around about now that they come.
　—If they come, he said.
　—I'm sure they will. They always have. Once, Dad saw them as they arrived. They flew straight in under the same roof tile as the year before.
　—Yes, you told me that.
　—In the old days people believed that a swallow building its nest in a house meant good luck for the people living there.
　—Yes, he said.
　He started walking up towards the house.
　He had carried a deckchair over to the apple tree and was lying back in it and looking up towards the forest. Suddenly, he heard her

call his name, loudly, as if something had happened. He got up and walked down towards the quay. She was sitting upright, her back to the fjord.

—What is it? he said.

She waved him closer.

—He was there again, that man, on the headland.

—So what? he said.

—I called out to you so he'd realize that I wasn't on my own.

He looked at her.

—Are you afraid that he's going to come and get you? he said.

—Oh, Martin. Really, she said.

He continued to look at her, then he turned and walked towards the back of the house.

They had eaten. A bank of cloud had built up in the west, and the low sun had disappeared behind it. She was sitting on the bench, reading; he was standing by the window looking out over the fjord.

—I'll open a bottle of wine, he said.

—Yes, she said, do that.

He uncorked the bottle and placed it on the table in front of her, along with two glasses. He filled her glass right up.

—That's a lot! She said.

—Yes, he said.

He took his own glass and sat down in the chair by the window.

—You seem to like sitting there, she said.

—Yes, he said.

She continued reading. After a while she looked up and said:

—Have you lowered the flag?

—Yes, he said.

—Have you? she said.

—No, he said.

—Why did you say yes? she said.

He didn't reply. Then he said:

—I'm going into town tomorrow to buy a pennant.

—Oh no, she said, not a pennant, they're so . . . we've never had a pennant.

He didn't reply.

She put down her book, got up and went into the kitchen. He heard her open and close the front door, then it was quiet. He took a gulp of wine, then another. He walked over to the table and filled his glass. He sat down and looked out over the fjord. After a while the door opened. He heard her pull out the drawer in the dresser, then push it back in. She came into the living room and sat down on the bench.

—Cheers, she said.

—Cheers, he said.

They drank.

—I took down the flag, she said. I'm sorry if it seems like I think you should be the one to do it.

He didn't reply.

—It's just that you always do it, she said. I didn't know you minded.

He didn't reply.

—You know, she said, I've never done it before. It was always Dad who did it. And then you. I've never been here on my own.

—No, I know, he said.

They had been sitting in silence for a long time. She was reading. He had finished his wine and refilled his glass. She put the book aside.

—I think I'm getting tired, she said. What time is it?

—Ten past ten, he said.

—Well, no wonder, she said. I was up so early.

—I'm going to turn in as well, he said.

—I don't mind if you stay up, she said.

She got to her feet.

—Okay, he said. Then I might as well stay up for a little while.

—After all, she said, you've still got half a glass of wine left.

—Yes, I can see that, he said.

When it had grown quiet in the house, he put on a windbreaker and went out the front door. He stood awhile on the quay, then he began to make his way over towards the headland. There was a pale crescent moon above the hill in the east. The air was still, and the sea gurgled almost soundlessly between the rocks by the shore.

He stood for a few minutes at the tip of the headland, then he walked quickly back to the house and in the front door. He opened another bottle of wine and sat down on the bench. It was past eleven o'clock. An hour later the bottle was empty. He put the two empty bottles beside each other on the table and stood up. He took off the windbreaker and threw it on the bench. He walked through the kitchen and up the stairs, opened the door to the bedroom and switched on the light. She was lying with her back to him. She didn't move. He went over to the closet and took out a woolen blanket. Mothballs fell down onto the floor. He slammed the closet door. She didn't move. He tugged the duvet off her.

—Martin! she said.

—Just lie there! he said.

—What is it? she said.

—Just lie there! he said.

Then he left.

She was lying on the quay. He saw her through the living room window. The wine bottles and glasses had been cleared away. The windbreaker lay on the bench.

He went outside and walked to the gate. He picked up the stone on the gatepost and flung it away, then he continued on up the dirt road.

He got into the car and started the engine. He backed the car out onto the road, then he reversed in again and turned off the engine. He sat quite still and looked straight ahead, for a long time.

He met her on his way back down to the house.

—Where have you been? she said.

—Just for a walk, he said.

—You could have told me, she said. I couldn't find you anywhere.

—I just went for a walk, he said.

—I was scared, she said.

—Why? he said.

—You know why, she said. Last night, and now this.

—Forget about last night, he said.

She looked at him.

—Forget about it, he said. I'd had too much to drink, it was nothing, I don't know what it was.

—I was beside myself, she said.

—Were you? he said.

He began to walk down towards the house. She followed after.

He sat at the end of the quay looking out over the fjord. She was lying behind him, sunning herself. She said:

—Isn't it a lovely spot.

—Certainly is, he said.

The Unseen

When Bernhard L. returned to his childhood home to attend his father's funeral, Marion gave him a rather awkward hug. It was a hot afternoon, and she had large, wet patches under her arms. So you came, she said. He told her he was tired from the journey and that he'd like to change. She had made up the attic room for him. The window was open and the sun flooded in across the floor. He took off all his clothes and lay down on the bed. He touched himself and tried to conjure up the image that had aroused him so intensely in the cramped train compartment, but wasn't able. Then he heard Marion coming up the stairs, and he got dressed. Sounds from the street outside could be heard from the window. Marion went back down the stairs. He opened the door of the closet and hung up his black suit.

When he went down to Marion a little later, she was sitting in the living room, crying. He assumed she hadn't heard him coming, but he wasn't sure, because she looked like he had caught her doing something wrong. He didn't know what to say. He walked to the window. He stood looking out at the small back garden. You were fond of him, he said. A black cat leapt up onto the fence. I should've been kinder to him, she said. Well, you were the one who looked after him, he said. The cat leapt from the fence up onto the roof of the old shed. She said: He could be so ... but he was in a lot of pain ... sometimes I almost wished ... there's a lot I regret. He lit a cigarette. I really didn't think he was going to die, she said. He asked how it happened. It took a while before she answered. He tipped the ash into one of the flowerpots. He was sitting in that chair, she said. I was in the kitchen. He asked me to come and read the newspaper for him. I told him I was in the middle of making dinner. He said that he wasn't hungry. Well I am, I said. It was quiet for a while, then he said: Are you going to be long. I didn't reply. I was annoyed at him. A little later, he called my name again, or said it rather, his voice wasn't particularly loud. But I didn't go in for another two or three minutes, and then he was dead.

Bernhard could picture his father sitting there, but he didn't feel anything. Marion began to cry again. He looked around for an ashtray to put out his cigarette. He walked into the kitchen and threw it into the sink. Then he drank a glass of water. The doorbell rang. Marion asked him to answer it. It was a woman. She looked at him and said: You must be Marion's brother. Yes, he said. She walked ahead of him into the living room. Marion wasn't there, he thought she must have gone to the kitchen to dry her eyes. The woman extended her hand, it was clammy, but he didn't mind. Camilla, she said. Bernhard, he said, I'll go and find Marion. Just then she came in. He stood looking at them for a while; they were so different in every perceptible way that he couldn't understand what they were doing with each other. Camilla was standing with her back to him, her clothes hugged her figure tightly, he thought: hasn't Marion realized that she's just being used? A moment later he dismissed the thought. Camilla turned to him and said something. He replied. She smiled and looked down. She works in a shop, he thought. Marion said something and went into the kitchen. He opened a window. Sit down, he said. She sat down. I'm sure Marion is happy you're here, she said. He laughed. He sat down opposite her. He asked if she had known his father. She gave a longwinded answer while she alternated between looking at her hands and at him. She had known him and yet not known him. She sat on the edge of the chair with her knees together and her hands folded on her thighs. He offered her a cigarette and gave her a light. He wondered which of them would be the first to mention there was no ashtray. Eventually he said: I'll go find an ashtray. He went into the kitchen. Marion was making up a plate of open sandwiches. She gave him a tiny ashtray. Haven't you got something bigger, he said. She tutted and gave him a large one. He walked into the living room. He asked Camilla how she and Marion knew each other. She told him. Marion came in and spread out a white tablecloth. Let me help you, said Camilla, but she didn't get up. No, no, said Marion. She set the table, and they ate. Camilla and Marion talked about a friend who'd had a child with spina bifida. It was seven in the evening. Bernhard noticed that Camilla kept glancing over at him. He sat picturing what she'd be like. Then a wasp came and landed on one of the sandwiches, and Camilla got up and went to the middle of the room. She said that she was allergic to wasp stings. Marion picked up a cheese sandwich and smacked it down on the bread the wasp was on. Bernhard laughed. Marion walked to the window and threw both slices into the garden. There, she said. Once again Bernhard laughed. Marion and Camilla sat down. Eat up, said Marion, Bernhard thought she looked happy. Camilla said that last time she was stung, she had to go to the A&E. Eat up, Bernhard, said Marion. He said he was full up. He got to his feet. He walked into the hall and up the stairs. The door to Marion's room was closed, he opened it and stood on the threshold looking in. The bed was unmade and there were clothes hanging over the backs of chairs. On the dresser was an enlarged photo in a frame; their mother and father standing on the stoop, they were smiling. He closed the door and went back downstairs.

A little later Camilla was ready to leave. Bernhard went up to the attic room. When he leaned out of the window, he could look down on the stoop right beneath. Camilla was standing facing the door; he could just see her hair and a little of her body. Marion was the one talking, but he couldn't catch what she was saying. No, no, not at all, said Camilla. She began walking down the steps. He pulled his head back. He watched her cut across the street and disappear into the alley between the watchmakers and the bakery. Bitch, he said to himself. He met his eyes in the mirror above the dresser, held his gaze for a while, quite long, his eyes began to narrow, and he said: Yeah, like that. Bitch.

He kicked off his shoes and flung himself on the bed, but soon got up again, went over to the door, and bent down to take a look at what he could see through the keyhole. He saw the top of the stairs and the door into what had been their parents' bedroom. He lay back down on the bed. Hardly any sounds came from in the window, only once in a while from cars driving past. It was ten minutes to eight. He thought: I need to ask for an extra pillow. He lit up a cigarette. There was no ashtray. He put one shoe on the bedside table, the sole facing up. I should probably go down to her, he thought. It's for her sake I'm here after all. I need to ask her for an extra pillow and an ashtray, in any case. Maybe she's waiting for me. Maybe she feels she can't go out because I'm here. He tipped the ash on the sole. He tried to think of something they could talk about. Then he heard a door opening, followed by footsteps on the stairs. He hurried over to the door and put his eye to the keyhole. As she passed his field of vision he saw her clearly, he saw her turn her head and look straight at him.

A little while later he went downstairs. He walked quietly, but he didn't creep down.

He went out the back garden and sat on a green folding chair by a round wrought-iron table. After a while he noticed the silence; nothing was stirring and there wasn't a sound to be heard. He felt a sudden sense of desertion, of confinement almost, and he got to his feet. He walked between the narrow flowerbed and the even narrower vegetable patch, over to the wooden fence. He stood with his back to the fence looking at the house and thought: there's no point in me being here. Just then he saw Marion; in the living room, standing a little back from the window; looking at him. She can't be certain I've seen her, he thought, letting his gaze wander further. Then he crouched down and started pulling up weeds from between the radishes, while glancing furtively at the door. She didn't come out. Then she must think I haven't seen her, he thought. He carried on weeding, and gradually felt content, almost a pleasure of sorts, at the sight of the clean, well-arranged miniature landscape springing up between his hands. He stopped snatching glimpses at the door, she could just come out, he was busy, he had a whole vegetable patch in front of him.

He reached as far as the lettuce when Marion came out together with a man carrying a bottle in his hand. Marion had three glasses. Bernhard straightened up. Marion told him he must say hello to Oskar. She placed the glasses on the round table. Bernhard nodded to Oskar, then went up and rinsed his hands under the outdoor water tap. He felt trapped. Marion poured wine into the glasses. Bernhard shook water from his fingers and walked over to the table. Oskar put his hand out. I'm wet, said Bernhard. Doesn't matter, said Oskar. He's a truck driver, thought Bernhard. Cheers, said Marion. They drank. Oskar took his jacket off, he had black, curly hair on his arms. Oskar and I are getting married, said Marion. Congratulations, said Bernhard. He tried to picture them, but wasn't able. Oskar is in the police, said Marion. Oh dear, said Bernhard. Oskar smiled. The death came at an opportune time then, thought Bernhard. He looked at Oskar and said: It's the first time I've raised a glass with a policeman. Isn't it a lovely evening, said Marion. Your vegetables need watering, said Bernhard. Oh dear, said Marion. The forecast is for more good weather, said Oskar. I'll water them, said Bernhard. They drank. Bernhard smoked. Oskar told them about a colleague of his who'd had a canoe stolen. Bernhard finished his drink, and Marion filled his glass. He stood up and went into the house, up to the second floor, and into the attic room. He stood there in the middle of the room letting time pass, then he went back down. He sat down and took a gulp of wine. He lit up a cigarette. Marion and Oskar talked. I have to remember to ask for an extra pillow, thought Bernhard. Then he thought: I'm not going to the funeral service. He had the same thought over again, several times. Marion stood up. I'm just going to ... she said. Do you think I could get an extra pillow? said Bernhard. Certainly, of course. She went into the house. Oskar scratched his arm. Have you known each other long? said Bernhard. Eight months, said Oskar. Then you knew my father? Yes. Well? No, not that well. He was ill, after all. He really didn't need to see anyone other than Marion. And you, of course. Bernhard laughed. Me, he said. Marion came back out, she had a jacket around her shoulders. Bernhard stood up. He went over to the old shed; there used to be a watering can there at one time. It was still there. He filled it from the water tap and walked over to the vegetable patch. He couldn't hear what Marion and Oskar were saying. The soil around the radishes turned black. He thought: he's probably brutal. And suddenly the image from the train compartment appeared to him quite clearly and Camilla stepped in and took the place of the anonymous woman. He wanted to bring the image with him up to the attic room, and he went to put the watering can back in the shed. Marion said: I suppose we should probably talk about tomorrow, Bernhard. Tomorrow? Yes, I've invited some people back here after the funeral, I hope that's alright with you. Yes, said Bernhard, that's the done thing, I suppose. He continued over to the shed, put down the watering can, lit up a cigarette, went back to the table, and sat down. Marion and Oskar chatted together. His wine glass was full, he drank. It had grown darker, their faces weren't completely distinct, he felt almost unseen. Almost free.

A little later Marion and Oskar went inside. Bernhard sat there smoking and sipping his wine. He thought: what lovely darkness. All of a sudden he felt a something against his right leg, and he gave a start and let out a little cry. He spilt some wine from his glass, and although at almost the very same moment he saw that it was a cat that had rubbed up against his trouser leg, the sudden anguish returned, as if to humiliate him, and he kicked out at the cat and felt and heard that he connected. He pushed the chair back and stood up, standing motionless for a moment, then he gave himself a shake, and began to walk back and forth on the paved path in front of the house. He said his own name to himself, over and over, like an incantation, and gradually he began to calm down. He came to a halt beneath the open living room window, listened out for voices, but it was quiet. He walked around to the north side of the house, to the gate onto the street, lifted the large latch and went out. He cut across the street and went into the alley between the watchmakers and the bakery, where he came to a halt and let his gaze sweep along the old houses leaning against one another. Then he turned and walked back the same way. Bitch, he said to himself. Bitch, bitch, bitch. He went in the gate. He lit up a cigarette. There was music coming from an open window in the house next door. He let the half-finished cigarette fall, stamped on it and thought: I have to remember the ashtray. He walked through the living room and into the kitchen. Marion was standing ironing a white blouse. He was afraid she would want to talk, so he said he was tired and was going to bed. She looked at him and smiled. You're not feeling great, are you? she said. Yes, he said, I'm just tired. He asked for an ashtray. She found one for him and said she had put an extra pillow on the bed. He placed his index finger on her forearm, and she looked at him, almost imploringly, he thought. Then he said good night and left.

During the service the following day he sat between Marion and his cousin Gustav. Marion held a handkerchief in her hand, but she didn't use it. The priest spoke about a dutiful father and the sorrow and loss of family and friends, which time would ease, but never quite heal, for such were the bonds of blood and the laws of love. As the closing psalm died out, Bernhard walked quickly from the chapel and out in the street. He lit up a cigarette. There were only three left in the pack, and he thought: I need to remember to buy some more. After a while Marion came out along with Oskar and Camilla. Bernhard looked the other way. He thought about how he had taken Camilla in the attic room the night before; she had resisted, but had been overcome. He began to walk along the foot-path. Marion called out to him. He stopped and turned. You can get a lift with Camilla, she said. I need to get cigarettes, he said. I'll get a taxi. She looked at him. Suit yourself, she said. He laughed. What is it, she said. Nothing, he said. He continued along the footpath. Suit yourself, he said to himself. Suit yourself, suit yourself. He stopped at a shop and bought two packs of cigarettes, then hailed a cab. The driver looked at him in the rearview mirror, and after a while he said: Party in the middle of the week? Yes, he replied. Wedding? Yes, my sister's getting married. They'll be raising hell, eh? Yes, raising hell. Bernhard shifted so close to the door that the driver's eyes disappeared from the mirror. He removed the black bowtie and put it in his pocket, then he undid the top button of his shirt. Actually, you can stop here, he said. I need to buy cigarettes. I'll walk the rest of the way. He paid. Have a good time, said the taxi driver. Bernhard laughed. Thanks, I will, he said.

The guests had arrived. Some of them came up to Bernhard, introduced themselves and offered their condolences. Their voices were low and they looked concerned. Bernhard lit up a cigarette. Marion smiled at him. Then she asked everyone to take a seat and have something to eat. Bernhard sat at the smallest table. Charlotte, his mother's sister, sat down beside him. I want to sit with you, she said. Do you, he said. Marion and Camilla went around with coffee. There were ashtrays on the table, and he put out his cigarette. Ah, well, said Charlotte. Bernhard held out the platter of open sandwiches to her. Oh, smoked salmon, she said, that's my favorite. Take two, said Bernhard. Camilla came and sat opposite him. Can I? said Charlotte. Of course, said Bernhard. I will then, she said. She tittered. You have to take what you want, said Bernhard and put the platter down in front of Camilla. He looked at her, met her gaze, she smiled. He thought: if you only knew. They ate. Did you know, Bernhard, said Charlotte, that I'm the oldest in the family now. Are you really, said Bernhard. So it'll be my turn next, she said. Now that's not necessarily true, he said. Oh, I think it is, she said. He didn't reply. Charlotte placed her hand on his arm. You mustn't think it matters, she said. Right, he said. He looked around him. Nobody appeared concerned anymore. He held the platter for Charlotte. This is the fourth funeral I've been to this year, she said. If you include my budgies. Bernhard laughed. Budgies? he said. Yes, they died two months ago. I had a female and a male, and then the eggs came, and then they ate their children, and then they died. From eating the eggs? he said. I suppose so, she said. It's unnatural to eat your own children. Bernhard laughed. Maybe they were related, he said. Who? she said. The two budgies, he said. Why? she said. No reason, he said. He thought he noticed Camilla staring at him, and he looked up to catch her eye, so quickly that she didn't manage to lower her own gaze. He smiled, and she smiled back. Next time I'll look at her breasts, he thought. Marion stood up and tapped her cup with a spoon. She said she wasn't going to give a speech, but just wanted to thank everyone for coming and for paying their respects. She didn't want to say anything about how she felt on a day like this, because then she'd only start to cry. But she wanted to once again thank everyone for coming, and hoped they enjoyed the simple spread. Then she sat down, and the guests sat in silence for a few moments, most of them with their heads lowered. Then they continued eating. What a lovely little speech, said Charlotte. Are you not going to say a few words? No! he said, curtly and loud enough that both Charlotte and Camilla looked at him. He felt his features stiffen. He crushed the half-finished cigarette out into the ashtray. Charlotte placed her hand on his arm, but he withdrew it. He lit up a fresh cigarette. He said his name to himself, several times. Camilla was sitting with her back straight, staring down at her plate. Oh, well, said Charlotte. Bernhard searched in vain for something to say. He picked up the platter and held it out to Charlotte. No, thank you, Bernhard, she said, I'm full up. She said it in such a kind, gentle way that he felt something swell up inside. And he suddenly remembered a rule he often heard her recite when he was a boy, and he turned to her and said: Do you remember ... There was a line, a kind of rule you used to quote when I was small and you were trying to comfort me, it began with "sigh little heart" ... Do you remember? Charlotte smiled. Yes, yes, I remember. Sigh little heart, but do not fret, you have a friend, you just don't know it yet. But you know ... it was probably ... I was so young then ... it was probably meant to comfort me just as much as you. It was when I was living with you all, you were, let me see, you were in third grade. You lived here, with us? said Bernhard. Yes, for about six months. I don't remember that, said Bernhard. How strange, said Charlotte, you must have been about nine. I've a very bad memory, said Bernhard. He lit up a cigarette. Do you know what, said Charlotte, I'd really like a cigarette right now. I don't smoke, only very occasionally. He held out the pack and then gave her a light. Would you like one? he said to Camilla. Thank you, she said. She looked at him while he gave her a light. He lowered his gaze. Bitch, he thought, just you wait. Camilla said: How long are you staying? Until tomorrow, he said, before adding: I don't know. Then he thought: Now!—and he looked at her breasts. Then he pushed his chair back and stood up. Without looking at anybody he then set the chair back and left. I did it, he thought, I did it. He went up to the attic room, took off the black suit and lay down on the bed, where he then took her by force.

Bernhard awoke from a dream. The sun was coming through the window at an angle. He got dressed and opened the door. It was completely quiet. He went downstairs. The back door was locked; he opened it and went out into the garden. The air was quite still, but there was a large cloud over the mountain in the east. He sat down at the wrought-iron table and kept an eye on it. It didn't draw closer. He thought: it's as though everything is as it was, as though nothing has happened.

A little later, he was still watching the cloud which wasn't drawing any closer, when he heard footsteps behind him. It was Marion. So this is where you are, she said. That cloud has been in the same spot for almost half an hour, he said. Some rain wouldn't go amiss, she said. It's not moving, he said. Marion put her finger in her mouth then held it up. There's no wind, she said. They sat in silence for a while. Would you like anything? said Marion. Like what? he asked. A glass of wine? she said. Yes, please, he said. She got up and went inside. He put his finger in his mouth then held it up. She probably wants to talk, he thought. She came out with a bottle of wine and two long-stemmed glasses. Lovely glasses, he said. Oskar gave them to me, she said. I'm certainly not going to sit here talking about Oskar, he thought. They drank. Bernhard lit up a cigarette. You left the table so suddenly, said Marion, was something the matter? No, he said, I just got such a headache. Aunt Charlotte said to give you her regards, said Marion. He laughed. She's the oldest in the family and the next one who's going to die, he said, and she's attending one funeral after another, and her budgies died because they ate their young. Marion smiled. She's sweet, she said, she looks like Mom. Bernhard said: She claimed she once lived here for six months when Mom was ill. That's right, said Marion, the year I started school. Mom was in the hospital. What was wrong with her?

I'm not sure exactly, something to do with her nerves. It's strange that I don't remember it, said Bernhard. You probably didn't miss her, said Marion. He didn't reply. He drank. Marion poured him more wine. Do you often get headaches? she said. No, he said. Or yes. Now and again. He threw away the cigarette and lit another. Look, he said, the cloud still hasn't moved. Camilla said that you're leaving tomorrow, said Marion. Yes, he said. That's a pity, she said. I need to get back to work, he said. He drank. That's good wine, he said. After a while he stole a glance at her; her eyes were downcast and she was shaking her head almost imperceptibly. Eventually, without looking up, she said: You don't want to talk, do you? I am talking, he said. You know what I mean, she said. He didn't reply. I was so happy when you came, she said, but maybe you didn't notice. He didn't reply. He didn't know what to say. Then he said: I only came for your sake. I thought ... He stood up. Don't go, said Marion. I'm not going, he said. What did you think? she said. He didn't reply. After a while he said: I can't help the way that I am. If I were to kill a person, for instance, I couldn't help it, but I'm not about to kill anyone, that's not how I am. Everything that I do, I do because that's how I am, and it's not my fault that I'm the way that I am. So other people can just say whatever they want. You know? He picked up his glass and drank. Then he lit up a cigarette. He walked over to the flowerbed, where he stood looking down at the dry soil. Then he looked at the cloud over the mountain; he thought it looked smaller. He turned to face Marion; she was leaning forward, turning the glass around and around on the table. He went and sat down. I can reach the end of my tether sometimes too, said Marion. Yes, he said. But from now on things should get better for you. She looked at him. Now that Dad is dead, I mean. Bernhard, really! she said. He laughed. All right, he said, we won't talk about it any more. I'll water the flowers.

Later, while they were eating dinner, a breeze made the curtains flap, and later as they were getting up from the table, there was a flash of lightning. Bernhard went out into the garden. The sun was shining, but the sky to the north was dark, and he heard distant thunder. He sat down at the garden table; he sat facing north, waiting for the rain. There was another lightning flash, and he thought: a bolt from the blue. Then he thought: but that's impossible, a lightning bolt from the blue is impossible. Just then Marion called his name. She was standing in the doorway. I'm just going to nip over to Camilla, she said, will you be here? He nodded. She waved and left. After a few minutes he got up and went inside. He called her name. Then he went upstairs into Marion's room. The bed was made, and there were no clothes hanging over the chairs. He went over to the dresser and stood looking at the photo of their parents. He thought: I look more like him than Mom. He remained standing in front of the photograph for a little while, he felt something stirring within which he thought would grow bigger, but it didn't. Then he pulled out the top drawer of the dresser, looked in it and pushed it back in. He just did it. He did the same with the next drawer and the second-to-last from the bottom. The bottom drawer was locked. There was no key. He pulled the second-to-last drawer right out and put it on the floor, and through the open space he could see a wallet, a stack of letters bound with string, two small boxes, a notebook and a spectacles case. And by itself, on the far right-hand side, a diary. He put his hand in and took out the letters; all of them were addressed to his father, he put them back again. He looked at the open door and listened, then he took out the wallet and opened it. There were seven one thousand kroner notes inside, and nothing else. He placed the wallet back exactly where it had been. He picked up the diary; under it lay a porn magazine. He opened the diary, it was Marion's. He put it back in its place and lifted the drawer up off the floor, stood holding it for a moment, it was full of underwear, and then put it back down again. He picked up the diary, leafed back in it, to the last entry she'd made. Wednesday, August 17th. Bernhard arrived, I really didn't think he'd come. I genuinely feel sorry for him, even though I don't really know if I've any reason to. He asked both Oskar and Camilla how well they knew Daddy. Camilla says there's almost something creepy about him, e.g. the way he laughs, but Oskar says he thinks he seems like a completely ordinary person. He probably wants to console me.

Bernhard closed the diary and put it back so that it covered the porn magazine, then he pushed the drawer back in and hurried out of the room and down the stairs. He stopped in the hall and lit up a cigarette. He opened the front door and stepped out onto the stoop. Like a completely ordinary person, he thought. Then he thought: they don't see me, there's no one who sees me. After a while some youths came walking down the street; he tossed the cigarette away and walked right through the house and out into the garden, where he sat down by the garden table. She'll probably bring Camilla along, he thought, so she doesn't have to be alone with me.

She didn't come back before the sun had gone down and he'd almost cleared the entire vegetable patch. The weeding had calmed him, his thoughts had led him to placid distractions beyond the present, and when he heard her coming, he looked up and smiled. She walked right over to him. What a lovely job you've done, she said in a low, warm voice, and he felt something surge within him. Yes, he said. She stood there, not saying anything else. The surging feeling had yet to subside. He couldn't look up. I'll soon be finished, he said. Yes, she said. Then she left.

She came back out as he was rinsing his hands under the water tap. She had a bottle of wine and two high-stemmed glasses. They sat in the gathering darkness, sipping wine and exchanged small words about small matters. Darkness descended. It didn't rain, said Bernhard. It doesn't matter, said Marion, you watered the beds. Yes, he said. He looked at her, her features were almost erased. She said: It's getting a bit chilly. I think I'll go inside. Are you going to sit here for a while? He nodded. A little longer, he said.

My Sister's Face

Late one afternoon in November, on my way upstairs to my place on the second floor, I noticed a shadow silhouetted against my front door. At once I realized there had to be someone standing between the door and the light bulb by the entrance to the attic, and I came to a halt. There had been a lot of break-ins in the area lately, some muggings too, probably due to widespread unemployment, and there was every reason to assume that the person standing motionless on the stairway up to the attic, didn't want to be seen. So I turned and began walking back down; it's been my experience that you should avoid drawing attention to someone who wants to stay hidden. I had only made it a little way down when I heard footsteps behind me; I was frightened, until the moment I heard a voice say my name. It was Oskar, my older sister's husband, and even though I didn't much care for him, I breathed, quite literally, a sigh of relief.

I walked back, and realizing right away that I couldn't avoid asking him in, I shook his hand. We hung up our coats on the hallstand, and then I went ahead of him into the living room and turned on the two free-standing lamps. He stood in the middle of the room looking around. He said he had never been here before. No, I don't suppose you have, I said. He asked how long I'd been living there. Six years, I said. Yes, that would be about right. He took off his glasses and rubbed one eye. I invited him to sit down, but he remained standing cleaning his glasses with a big handkerchief while he squinted half-blindly at the room. Then he put his glasses back on. You do have a phone, he said. Yes, I said. But you're not in the telephone book, he said. No, I said. I sat down. He looked at me. I asked him if he'd like a cup of coffee. No thanks, he said, besides he had to be on his way soon. He sat down opposite me. He said my sister had sent him, she wanted me to visit her, she was at home with a sprained ankle and had something she wanted to discuss with me, he didn't know what, she hadn't said, actually yes, he said, apparently something to do with when you were kids, and when he told her she could easily write to me, she'd become hysterical, unscrewed the top off a tube of glue and emptied its contents over the carpet. A tube of glue? I said. Yes, he said, photo glue, she'd been gluing photographs back onto the pages of an old album. He took off his glasses again and rubbed his eye, then he took out his handkerchief again and cleaned the lenses. I'll ring her, I said. Right, he said, then at least she'll know I've been here. Actually, he continued, if you give me your phone number, then she can ring you if anything comes up, then I'll be spared the journey halfway across town to call on you. I didn't want to give him my number, but so as not to insult him, I said I couldn't remember it. He studied me through the thick lenses, I was a bit uncomfortable, I usually only lie in self-defense, so perhaps it's possible to tell I'm lying just by looking at me, I felt that he could tell in any case, and I said I never used it, after all you don't ring yourself very often. No, of course not, he said, and the way he said it annoyed me, I felt I'd been put in my place, and I went out and fetched cigarettes from my coat pocket. I'm afraid I don't have much to offer you other than a cup of coffee, I said. He didn't reply. I sat down and lit a cigarette up. You're lucky, you are, he said. Oh? I said. Living here all by yourself, he said. Oh, I don't know, I said, even though I agreed. Sometimes I don't know what to do with myself, he said. I didn't reply. Right, I'll be off, he said, getting to his feet. I felt a little sorry for him, so I said: Things aren't great between you? No, he said. He walked towards the door. I followed. I held out his coat. He said: I'm sure if you ring it'll make her happy. She says you're the only person who cares about her.

She must have been sitting within reach of the phone because she picked it up straight away. I said who I was. Oh Otto, she said, I'm so happy to hear from you. She seemed sincere and in no way tense and the subsequent conversation progressed in a relaxed, friendly tone. After a while she invited me to hers, and I said yes. Then she said: Because you haven't forgotten us, have you? Forgotten you? I said. No, she said, us, you and me. No, I said. Are you coming tomorrow? she said. I hesitated. Yes, I said. Around one? she said. Yes, I said.

After I'd replaced the receiver, I was in high spirits, excited almost, a feeling I often get when I've finished something difficult, and I celebrated by pouring myself a quarter glass of whisky, something I wouldn't usually do at that time of the day. The feeling of elation endured, thanks now to the whisky perhaps, and I treated myself to another glass. At almost half past seven, I locked the front door and went to The Bigwig, a dive that doesn't live up to its name, but where I have a beer or two now and again.

Karl Homann was sitting there, a man my own age who lives in the area, with whom I have a somewhat forced relationship, because he once saved my life. Fortunately he wasn't sitting on his own, so when he asked me to take a seat I felt I could take the liberty of finding a table to myself. I went to the very back of the premises. The fact that I had mustered up the courage to refuse his invitation had me so flustered it was only after I sat down that I noticed Marion, a woman with whom I'd had a not entirely painless relationship. She was sitting three tables away. She was flicking through a newspaper and it was possible she hadn't seen me yet. I didn't necessarily have to have seen her either, and I ordered my beer and awaited developments. There was however, something unbearable about the situation, and I tried to catch her eye. After a little while she glanced up from her paper and straight at me, and I knew then she'd spotted me ages ago. I smiled at her and raised my glass. She raised hers too, then folded her paper and came over to me. I got to my feet. Otto, she said and gave me a hug. Then she said: Can I join you? Of course, I said, but I'll be off soon, I'm on my way to my sister's. She brought her glass. She seemed to be in fine form. She said it was good to see me, and I said that it was good to see her. She said she often thought about me. I didn't reply, even though I'd also thought about her, albeit with mixed emotions, not least due to her sexual needs which I hadn't managed to satisfy and which on one occasion, the last, had led her to exclaim that sex was not a church service. To change the subject I asked how things were, and we chatted until I'd drained my glass and said I had to be off. Then she'd go too, she said. As we were getting to our feet, she said: If you hadn't been on your way to visit your sister, would you have come back to my place? I'd have been tempted, I said. Ring me sometime, she said. Yes, I said.

She walked with me to the bus stop, and once there she pressed up against me and whispered some lewd, suggestive words which put my body in a quandary, and well, if the bus hadn't come, but it did, and she said: Ring. Yes, I said.

I got off at the next stop, and bucked by the self-esteem Marion's advances had stirred in me—she is a beautiful woman—I headed straight for the closest bar. But I only got as far as the door; when I opened it and saw the crowd of people and heard the noisy music, my nerve failed. It's a situation I'm well used to, the frightening sense of alienation in an unfamiliar place, and I closed the door and went home.

Later that night I was awoken by a dream no doubt influenced by said self-esteem that Marion's pass evoked in me. It was an intensely erotic dream, and unlike the typical dream, where the woman's face—or women's faces—are unknown or not even missing, this woman's features suddenly appeared, clearly, without diminishing my desire. It was my sister's face.

She opened the door before I had managed to ring the bell. She was leaning on two crutches. I saw you coming, she said. So I see, I said. She hugged me and lost one of the crutches doing so. I bent down to pick it up. Hold me up, can you? she said, putting her arm around my shoulder. I did, that is to say, she held herself up on me. She hobbled along beside me into the living room and sat herself down at the already-set coffee table. After I'd hung up my coat and gone back in, we ate sandwiches and talked about her foot. I took a furtive glance at the carpet, but couldn't see a trace of any photo glue.

We'd been talking a while about this and that, when she said: You're more and more like Dad. Thinking she knew what kind of relationship I'd had with him, I took slight exception to this, but I didn't say anything. I got up to look for an ashtray. What are you doing? she said. Looking for an ashtray, I said. She told me where I could find one, and I went to the kitchen. When I went back in, she said she'd been thinking about me a lot lately, about us, and how it was a pity we didn't see so much of each other, since we used to be so close. Well, I said, everyone's got their lives to live. Do you ever miss me? she said. Of course, I said. If you only knew how lonely I feel sometimes, she said. Yes, I said. You're lonely too, she said, I know you are, I know you. It's a long time since you knew me, I said. You haven't changed, she said. Yes, I have, I said. In what way? she said. I didn't reply. Then I said: You just said yourself that I'm getting more and more like Dad. What did you mean by that, by the way? There's something about the way you smile, she said, and you sway when you sit just like he did. Did he sway, I said, I don't remember that. That's strange, she said. I guess I didn't look at him as much as you did, I said. What do you mean? she said. What I said, I said. I didn't like looking at him. There was something unsavory about him. Oh Christ, she said. We sat in silence for a while; then I became aware that I was swaying my torso and I straightened up and leaned back in the chair. Eventually she said: There's a bottle of sherry in the bottom corner cupboard, could you go and get it please. And two glasses, if you'd like some too. On the way to the cupboard I decided to only get one glass, but I changed my mind. I poured her a large one and myself a little one. You've never said that before, she said. No, I said, let's talk about something else. Cheers. Cheers, she said. I drained the glass. You didn't give yourself much, she said. I don't drink in the middle of the day, I said. Me neither, she said. I poured myself some more. I didn't know what we were going say. I looked at my watch. Don't look at your watch, she said. Where's Oskar? I said. At his mother's. He's always at his mother's on Saturdays. He never gets home before five, so relax. I am relaxed, I said. Are you?

she said. Course, I said. Good, she said, can you give me a little more sherry? I poured her some, but not as much as the last time. More, she said. I topped up her glass. Cheers, she said. I drained my glass. Help yourself, she said. I remembered what she had said to Oskar, that I was the only person who cared about her, and with a sudden and almost triumphant feeling of freedom, I filled my glass up to the brim. She looked at me, her eyes were shining. You're staring at me, she said. Yes, I said. Do you remember how I called you big brother? she said. I nodded. And you called me sister, she said. I took my glass and drank. She did the same. I remembered. Have you got a girlfriend at the moment? she said. No, I said. No one good enough for you? she said. Don't make fun of me, I said. I'm not making fun of you, she said. I prefer living on my own, I said. You could still have a girlfriend, she said. I didn't reply. After all, you're a man, she said. I didn't reply. I got up and went to the toilet. I placed the plug in the sink and turned on the cold-water tap. I put my hands into the water and held them there until they hurt, then I dried them and went back into the living room. I sat down and said what I had been thinking: I prefer women who don't make any demands of me, but who give, take and go. She didn't say anything. I lit a cigarette. And you say you're not lonely, she said, before adding: Big brother. I looked at her; she was sitting with her face half-turned and her lips parted; there wasn't a sound in the room and no sound from outside; the silence lasted and lasted. What if, she said. What if what, I said. No, she said. Yes, I said. But Otto, she said, you don't know what I—what do you think I was thinking of? I was just about to say, at that moment I almost had it in me. Instead I said: No, how should I know. She took her glass and held it out to me. It's empty, she said. Say when, I said. No, she said. I filled the glass right up. We're drinking a lot for two people who don't drink during the day, I said. There are exceptions, she said. Yes, I said, there are exceptions to everything. Are there? she said. She wasn't looking at me. Yes, I said. There was a sound of somebody at the front door. Oh no, she said. I got to my feet. It was a reflex action. Don't go, she said. I sat down. Oskar appeared in the doorway; he was walking while supporting himself on my sister's crutch. He halted. I could see by his face that he didn't know I was there. Hello, Oskar, I said. Hello, he said. He looked at my sister and said: Your crutch was lying by the door. I'm aware of that, she said. Sorry, he said and let the crutch fall to the floor. Now what's the point of that? she said. He didn't reply. He kicked the crutch against the wall with the tip of his shoe, and then he walked into the kitchen. He closed the door behind him. Don't go, please, she said. I'm going, I said. For my sake, she said. I'm not up to it, I said. Oskar came from the kitchen. He glanced at me. I didn't know you were here, he said. I'm just leaving, I said. Not on my account, he said. No, I said. He walked across the room and through a door. I looked at my sister; she stared straight at me and said: You're a coward, I'd forgotten what a coward you were. I got to my feet. Yes, just go, she said, just go. I went over to her. What did you say? I said. That you're a coward, she said. I hit her. Not hard. No, I don't think I hit her particularly hard. She cried out all the same. At almost exactly the same moment I heard Oskar open the door; he must have been standing right behind it, listening. I didn't turn around. I didn't hear any steps. I looked at the wall. I only heard the sound of my own breathing. Then my sister said: Otto is just leaving. Oskar didn't reply. I heard the door being closed. I looked at my sister, met her gaze; there was something in it I didn't understand, something gentle. I saw she wanted to say something. I looked away. Forgive me, big brother, she said. I didn't reply. Go now, she said, but ring me, won't you? Yes, I said. Then I turned and left.

Where the Dog Lies Buried

At the beginning of March, winter loosened its grip. A mild, almost warm wind blew in from the southeast, and the deep snow that had lain since before Christmas, began to subside and melt.

One Friday afternoon, three days after the thaw set in, Jakob E. fetched the snow shovel from the garage and went around to the back of the house where he began shoveling snow away from the basement flaps. The last few times he had been in the basement, he'd noticed a faint, but unpleasant odor and he didn't know where it was coming from. Now he was going to open the flaps and the door and give the basement a proper airing out after the winter.

After a while he put down the shovel and opened the flaps, and the sight and smell hit him simultaneously. He cried out and let go of the handle, and the flap closed with a bang. He let out another cry and a shiver went through him, then he took a few quick steps backwards, as if being pursued.

Little by little his panic abated, and he thought: but that's impossible. He stood staring fixedly at the basement flap and thought again and again: that's impossible. A dead dog, that's impossible.

But it was there, the decomposed, stinking carcass of a large dog with a dark coat. And he had to do something about it. He just didn't know what.

He left the shovel, walked past the garage and into the house. Erna was sitting by the kitchen table reading the paper, she didn't look up. He sat down opposite her and lit up a cigarette. Erna smiled at something she was reading. He said:

—There's a dead dog under the basement flap.

—Under . . . A dead dog?

—It's been there since before Christmas.

—No.

—I don't know what to do. The stench alone. What's more, it's big.

—Since before Christmas? Oh God.

—Before the snow.

—Oh God. Jakob. What'll you do?

—I don't know.

He got to his feet. He walked to the window. After a while he asked:

—Do we have any bleach?

—Under the sink.

He got it out and walked outside. He went into the garage. He took down a coiled clothesline from a hook on the wall and went around to the back of the house. He tied one end of the line to the handle of the flap. It's only a dead dog, he thought. He backed up two or three meters, pulled the line taut and tugged. The flap opened. He walked past the open basement steps, took hold of the shovel and began ladling snow down the opening. Only when he was sure the cadaver was buried, did he go over and look down. Then he went to fetch the bleach, but as he was about to unscrew the cap, he noticed the neighbor standing at the kitchen window looking at him. For a moment he stood there at a loss, as though caught in the act. Then, with hard-earned composure and without looking in the direction of the house next door, he took the shovel and the bleach, placed them in the garage and went into the house.

Erna wasn't in the kitchen. He sat down and lit up a cigarette. Martin? he thought. Before the snowfall. Martin? He heard Erna come down the stairs.

—Have you got rid of it? she asked.

—No. Holt was standing at the window. I'll wait till it's dark.

—Do you not have to notify the police?

He didn't answer.

—After all, someone must be missing it.

—Let me deal with this in my own way, please.

—Yes, but somebody has done this. To us.

—We don't know that. Who'd do a thing like that?

—Yes, who'd do a thing like that. In any case, it didn't walk down by itself. Oh God!

—What is it?

—Imagine it, oh God, imagine it was locked in.

—Don't get hysterical.

—I'm not hysterical. But I don't understand why you're so against telling the police.

—I've told you, I'll deal with this my own way, and we're not going to talk about it anymore.

He got to his feet. He walked out of the kitchen, through the hall and down into the basement. He took an old plastic tablecloth down from the shelf over the workbench and cut a hole in each corner. After that he cut a five or six meter long rope into four equal lengths and tied them through each hole. Then he went over to the basement window and looked out. Night was falling, in a half hour it would be dark enough. He saw me, he thought, but from that angle he couldn't see the dog.

He picked up the tablecloth, walked up the basement stairs and out to the garage. He got into the car and lit up a cigarette. When he thought it was dark enough, he took the bleach and walked over to the entrance to the basement steps. There was no one at the kitchen window. He splashed the bleach over the snow covering the dog's cadaver, then went back to the garage and got the shovel and the plastic tablecloth. He maneuvered the dog to the side of the steps with the shovel, after which he spread the tablecloth out beside it. Then he slipped the shovel in under the dog's body and turned it over onto the tablecloth. The carcass came into view, the stench hit him, and he vomited.

Later, when he had spaded some more snow over the dog, he undid the clothesline from the handle on the flap and made a loop at the end. He passed the four lengths of rope on the plastic tablecloth through the loop and tied them off. There was no one at the kitchen window. He began to pull at the line, and the tablecloth took on the shape of a seine around the dog. It was easier than he anticipated, and the tablecloth held. He hauled it through the snow, down to the wooden fence at the end of the garden, then he fetched the shovel and spaded a half meter of snow over it. I did it, he thought.

A half hour later, after showering and brushing his teeth, he went into the living room. Erna was sitting watching TV.

—It's done, he said.

She didn't reply. He sat down. All right then, he thought. He lit up a cigarette. A minute passed.

—Where did you put it? she asked.

—Down in the vegetable patch. I shoveled snow over it.

—And when the snow melts?

—Then I'll bury it.

—In the vegetable patch?

—Yes.

—No Jakob, I don't want it under the vegetables.

—Where else can it go? Do you want me to dig up the lawn?

—Do what you want, but I don't want it under the vegetables.

—I've never heard anything so stupid.

—I don't care if you haven't. And by the way I still think you should report it to the police.

—Stop nagging about the police, for God's sake!

—What kind of way is that to talk to me, Jakob.

—I'll talk how I please. I stressed with that damned cadaver until I threw up, and all you do is pester me about the police.

He stood up abruptly and left the room.

—Jakob! She called out after him. He didn't reply. He went upstairs to the bedroom, but he soon came out, he had no reason to be in there. He didn't know where to go. He sat at the top of the stairs. He tried to remember when exactly it was that Martin left, but he wasn't able.

He heard the telephone ring, and when Erna took it, he stood up and went down to the kitchen. The living room door was open, but he couldn't hear what she was saying. He drank a glass of water. Then he let the glass fall to the floor, but it didn't break. He picked it up and dropped it again. He put some force behind it, but not much. The glass broke, but not into as many pieces as he'd imagined. He fetched the dustpan and the broom and began sweeping it up. Erna didn't appear. He went into the living room to find an old newspaper. Erna was sitting on the sofa, she'd switched off the TV. He took the paper and went back into the kitchen. Then wrapped the pieces of glass up in the paper and put it in the rubbish bin. From where he was standing, he could see Erna through the doorway. She was sitting on the edge of the sofa, staring right ahead, her lips pressed together. He turned off the light and lit up a cigarette. If she turned her head she'd be able to see him standing in the darkness smoking. She turned her head. He finished smoking the cigarette and went in to her.

—Is there nothing on TV? he asked

—Just a concert, she replied.

He picked up the newspaper on the coffee table and sat down.

—I just have to say, she said,—that no matter how unpleasant you thought it was dealing with that dog, you shouldn't have taken it out on me. You know how it makes me feel when you shout at me.

He lit up a cigarette.

—I just had to say it, she said,—and now I have. I'll go and make us some coffee.

She got up and went into the kitchen. He sat with the paper in his lap listening to the sounds she made. He let the paper slip onto the floor and put out his cigarette. Then he hunched up his shoulders and pressed his palms so hard against his ears that all he could hear was the hum inside his own head. He didn't notice her coming back in, but then he became aware that she was standing looking at him.

—What's wrong with you? she said.

—Nothing. I've got such a humming in my head.

—You think it might have been Martin, don't you?

—Martin? What? Which Martin?

—Your Martin. That's why you wouldn't report it, isn't it? You were afraid it might have been Martin.

He got to his feet. He met her eyes, and she took a step back.

—What the fuck are you saying!

—But . . .

—What the fuck are you saying!

—I didn't mean . . . I'm sorry. You're frightening me. Please don't frighten me. Jakob . . . No!

He withdrew his hand. He turned around. He went into the kitchen. The water for the coffee was boiling, he turned off the hob. The coffee cups, jug of cream, and sugar bowl were on the tray on the kitchen bench. He stood looking at it for a while, then he nodded, several times. He got the instant coffee from the cupboard, spooned some into the cups, poured water in and carried the tray into the living room. Erna was sitting on the sofa, her eyes downcast. She had her arms wrapped around her, as if she was cold. Jakob put down the coffee cup, the cream and the sugar bowl in front of her. She didn't look up. He switched on the TV, there was a thriller on. He sat back in the chair and lit up a cigarette. After a while Erna got to her feet and went up to the bedroom, he could hear her footsteps. She didn't come back down.

The next evening, Jakob laid a large tarpaulin over the mound of snow by the wooden fence, and when the ground thawed, he buried the dog in the vegetable patch. Erna didn't say a word, but when spring came, the vegetable patch lay fallow.

The Nail in the Cherry Tree

Mom was standing in the small back garden, a long time ago now, I was a lot younger then. She was hammering a long nail into the trunk of the cherry tree, I saw her from the second-story window, it was a humid, overcast day in August, I saw her hang the hammer up on the long nail, then she walked to the fence at the end of the garden where she stood, quite motionless, looking out over the extended treeless plain, for a long time. I walked downstairs and out into the garden, I didn't like her just standing there, there was no telling what she'd see. I went over and stood beside her. She touched my arm, looked up at me and smiled. She had been crying. She smiled and said: I can't take it, Nicolay. No, I said. We walked up to the house and into the kitchen, and just then Sam arrived. He complained about the heat, and Mom put on the kettle. The windows were open. Sam was telling Mom about a bed that had given his wife a sore back, and I went upstairs, up to Sam's room, as it was called, since he was the eldest, and the first one to have one to himself. I stood in the middle of Sam's room and let time pass, then I went back down. Sam was talking about an outboard engine. Mom put some sugar in her tea and stirred and stirred with the spoon. Sam wiped his neck with a blue handkerchief, I couldn't stand to look at him, I told Mom I was off to buy tobacco, and I took my time, but when I got back he was still sitting there. He talked about the funeral, about how the priest had found just the right words. You think? said Mom. I asked Sam how old his son was. He looked at me. Seven, he said, you know that. I didn't answer, he continued looking at me, and Mom got up and brought the cups to the sink. So he's going to start school, I said. Of course, he said, everyone starts school when they're seven. Yes, I replied, I know. I got up and walked into the hall, up the stairs and into Sam's room, my head felt like it was at the bottom of a lake. I put the tobacco pouch into my suitcase, locked it and pocketed the key. No,

I said to myself. I opened the suitcase again, took out the tobacco pouch, took the other pouch out of my pocket, and walked down to the kitchen with both of them in my hand. Sam stopped talking. Mom was drying the dishes with a red check tea towel. I sat down, put both pouches on the table, and rolled a cigarette. Sam looked at me. There was complete silence, for a long time, then Mom began to hum. What about you, Sam said, you're still at the same thing. Yes, I said. I'll never get it, he said. Grown men writing poetry. Not doing anything else, I mean. Now, now, Sam, said Mom. But I don't get it, said Sam. That's understandable, I said. I got up and went out to the garden. It was too small for me, I climbed over the fence and began walking across the plain. I wanted to be visible, but from a distance. I walked about eighty, ninety, maybe one hundred meters, then I came to a halt and turned around. I could see half of Sam's car to the right of the house. The air was quite still. I hardly felt a thing. I stood looking at the house and the car, for a long time, maybe a quarter of an hour, maybe longer, until Sam drove away, I didn't see him, only the car. Mom came out into the garden immediately after, and when I saw that she'd seen me, I walked back. She said Sam had to be off, he said to give you his regards. You don't say, I said. He is your brother, she said. Ah Mom, I said. She shook her head and smiled. I asked if she wanted to have a rest, and she did. We went in. She stopped in the middle of the room. She opened her mouth wide, as if she was wanted to scream, or as though she needed air, then she closed it again and said, in a feeble voice: I don't think I can get over it, Nicolay. I just want to die. I put my arms around her frail, bony shoulders. Mom, I said. I just want to die, she repeated. Yes, Mom, I said. I led her to the sofa, she was crying, I laid the blanket over her legs, her eyes were squeezed shut and she wept loudly, I sat on the edge of the sofa, looked at the tears and thought of Dad, that she must have loved him. I placed my hand on her bosom, in a way I was aware of what I was doing, and she stopped squeezing her eyes, but didn't open them. Oh Nicolay, she said. Sleep, Mom, I said. I didn't take my hand away. After a while, her breathing was steady, and I got up, went into the hall, up the stairs and into Sam's room. The train wasn't leaving for almost five hours, but I was sure she would understand. I packed my suitcase, putting the black suit in last. My head felt like it was in a large room. I went down the stairs and out the door. I walked the whole way to the station, it was quite far, but I had plenty of time. I walked along thinking that she must have loved Dad, and that Sam . . . that she probably loved him too. And I thought: it doesn't matter.

A Great Deserted Landscape

I'd been helped out onto the veranda. My sister Sonja had placed cushions under my feet, and I was in hardly any pain. It was a warm day in August, my wife's funeral was about to take place, and I was lying in the shade looking up at the pale blue sky. I was unaccustomed to such bright light, and on one of the occasions Sonja came to check on me, I had tears in my eyes. I asked her to fetch my sunglasses, I didn't want her to misunderstand. She went to find them. It was only the two of us; the others were at the funeral service. She came back and put the sunglasses on me. I formed a kiss with my lips. She smiled. I thought: if she only knew. The sunglasses were so dark that I could look at her body without her noticing. When she was gone I looked up at the sky again. From somewhere quite far off I could hear the sound of hammering, it was reassuring, I never like when it's completely silent. I once said that to Helen, my wife, and she replied that it was due to feelings of guilt. You couldn't talk to her about that kind of thing, she'd immediately start prying. _

When I'd been lying there for quite some time, and the blows of the hammer had long since ceased, it suddenly grew a lot darker around me, and before I realized that it was due to the combined effect of a cloud and the dark sunglasses, I was seized by an inexplicable feeling of anxiety. It passed almost immediately, but something remained, a feeling of emptiness or desolation, and when Sonja came out to check on me a little later, I asked for a pill. She said it was too early. I insisted, and she removed my sunglasses. Don't do that, I said. I closed my eyes. She put them back on. Are you in a lot of pain? Yes, I said. She left. She returned soon after with a pill and a glass of water. Propping me up by my uninjured shoulder, she put the pill in my mouth and held the glass to my lips. I could smell her scent.

Not long after, my mother, my two brothers and my sister-in-law came back from the funeral. And Helen's father, her two sisters, and an aunt I hardly knew, arrived a little after that. Everyone came over and said a few words to me. The pill was beginning to take effect, and I lay hidden behind the dark sunglasses feeling like a godfather. I didn't feel it necessary to say too much, naturally enough everyone credited me with profound grief, there was no way they could know I was lying there feeling immense indifference. And when Helen's father came up to me and said something or other, I felt something approaching satisfaction thinking about how, now that Helen was dead, he was no longer my father-in-law, and Helen's sisters were no longer my in-laws either.

A little later my brother's wife and Helen's sisters began putting out plates and cutlery on the long garden bench below the veranda, and every time they went past me on the way into the living room, they nodded and smiled, even though I pretended not to see them. Then I must have dozed off, because the next thing I remember is the buzz of conversation down in the garden, and I could see their heads, nine heads hardly moving. It was a peaceful scene, those nine heads in the shade of the big birch tree, and at the end of the table, facing me: Sonja. After a while I raised my arm, to attract her attention, but she didn't see me. Right after that my youngest brother stood up and made his way towards the veranda. I closed my eyes and pretended to be asleep. I heard him stop up for a moment as he passed me, and I thought: we are completely helpless.

Eventually they got up from the table, and the entire time they were all, with the exception of Mom and Sonja, getting ready to go, I lay with my eyes closed, pretending to sleep. Then Mom emerged from the living room and came over to me. I smiled at her, and she asked if I was hungry. I wasn't. Are you in pain? she asked. No, I said. What about on the inside? she said. No, I said. Well, she said and fixed the sheet I had over me, even though it was straight. Would you sooner be off home? I asked. Why? she replied, do you not want me here? Of course, I said, I just thought you might miss Dad. She didn't reply. She went over and sat on the wicker sofa. Just then Sonja appeared. I removed my sunglasses. She had a wine glass in her hand. She gave it to Mom. I'd like one as well, I said. Not with pills, she said. Don't be silly, I said. Just one glass then, she said. She left. Mom sat looking out over the garden, the wine glass in her hand. Is this all yours now? she asked. Yes, I said, ownership by conveyance. There'll be a lot of emptiness, she said. I didn't reply, I wasn't sure what she meant. Sonja came out with two glasses, she placed one down on the nest of tables beside Mom. She came out to me with the other, held me by the shoulder, and brought the glass to my lips. She bent over more than the last time, and I could glimpse her breasts. As she was taking the glass away, our eyes met, and I don't know, maybe she saw something she hadn't noticed before, because something flashed in her eyes, something resembling anger. Then she smiled and went over to sit beside Mom. Cheers, Mom, she said. Yes, said Mom. They drank. I put on my sunglasses. Nobody spoke. I didn't find it a very comfortable silence, I wanted to say something, but I didn't know what. There are no birds here, said Sonja. There are none around our place either, said Mom. Apart from seagulls. There used to be swallows, lots of swallows, but they're gone now. That's a pity, said Sonja. What's that down to? That's what no one can figure out, said Mom. Then they didn't say anything else for a while. Now we can't tell if it's going to be nice or if it's going to rain anymore, said Mom. You could just listen to the weather forecast, said Sonja. You can't rely on them, said Mom. In the Mediterranean, swallows fly low even if it isn't going to rain, said Sonja. Well then they must be a different type of swallow, said Mom. No, said Sonja, they're the same type. That's odd, said Mom. Sonja didn't say anything else. She drank her wine. Is that true what Sonja's saying? asked Mom. Yes, I said. Jesus, you never believe anything I say, said Sonja. I think it ought to be beneath your dignity to swear on a day like today, said Mom. Sonja drained her glass and stood up. You're right, she said, I should wait until tomorrow. Now you're being mean, said Mom. And to think I was such a good-natured child, said Sonja. She came over and helped me to more wine. She didn't hold my head high enough, and some of it ran out of the corner of my mouth and down my chin. She wiped me rather roughly with a corner of the sheet, her lips were tightened in anger. Then she went into the living room. What's got into her? said Mom. She's an adult, Mom, I said, she doesn't want to be told off. But I'm her mother, she said. I didn't reply. I only want what's best for her, she said. I didn't reply. She started crying. What's wrong, Mom? I said. Nothing's the way it used to be, she said, everything is so ... strange. Sonja came back out. I'm going for a walk, she said. I think she saw that Mom was crying, but I'm not sure. She left. She's so pretty, I said. What good is that, said Mom. Oh, Mom, I said. You're right, she said, I don't know what I'm saying. It's okay if you want to go home, I said, Sonja's here after all. She started crying again, louder this time, and more uncontrollably. I let her cry for a while, long enough, I thought, then I said: Why are you crying? She didn't reply. I started to get annoyed, I thought: what the fuck have you got to cry about? Then she said: Your father's met someone. Met someone? I said. Dad? I wasn't planning to tell you, she said. It's not as if you don't have enough sorrows of your own. I've no sorrows, I said. How can you say such a thing? she said. I didn't reply. I lay there thinking about that skinny little man, my father, who at the age of sixty-three ... a man I'd never credited with more libido than was strictly necessary to sire me and my siblings. An image of him, naked between a woman's thighs, flashed before me. It was extremely unpleasant. Mom brought the empty glasses inside, but she soon came back, so I could tell she wanted to talk. She stood with her back to me looking out at the garden. What are you going to do? I asked. What can I do, she replied, he says I can do what I want, so there's nothing I can do. You can stay here, I said. I could see by her back that she had started crying again, and perhaps because she didn't want me to see her, she began walking down the veranda steps. She likely had tears in her eyes, and she must have stumbled, because she lost her balance and fell forwards, and disappeared from my view. I called out to her, but she didn't answer. I called out several more times. I tried to get up but there was nothing I could hold on to. I turned over on my side and eased one leg, in plaster, out over the side of the lounger, supported myself by my elbow and managed to sit up. Then I saw her. She was lying face down in the gravel. I lifted my other leg, also in plaster, off the lounger. My shoulder and arm hurt most. I couldn't walk with both legs in casts, so I slid down onto the floor. I inched my way over to the steps. There wasn't a great deal I could do, but I couldn't just leave her lying there. I edged my way down the steps and over to her. I tried to turn her over on her side, but wasn't able. I slid my hand beneath her forehead. It was moist. The gravel cut into the back of my hand. I had no strength left. I lay down beside her. Then she moved a little. Mom, I said. She didn't reply. Mom, I said. She groaned and turned her face to me, she was bleeding and looked frightened. Where does it hurt? I said. Oh no! she said. Just lie still, I said, but she rolled onto her back and sat up. She looked at her bloodied knees and began picking pebbles from the cuts. Oh no, oh no, she said, how did I . . . You fainted, I said. Yes, she said, everything went black. Then she turned and stared at me. William! she said. What have you done! Oh my dear, what have you done! There, there, I said. I was lying in a painful position, and with my one good arm I inched my way onto the lawn. I lay there on my back and closed my eyes. My shoulder ached, it felt as if the fracture had recurred. Mom was talking, but I didn't have the energy to answer. I felt I'd done my bit. I heard her get to her feet. I didn't want to open my eyes. She groaned. Come and sit on the grass, I said. What about you? she said. I'm fine, I said, come and sit down, Sonja's bound to be back soon. I looked at her. She could hardly walk. She sat down gingerly beside me. I think I need to lie down a little, she said. We lay in the sun, it was hot. You mustn't fall asleep, I said. No, I know that, she said. Then we didn't say anything for a while. Don't say anything to Sonja about Dad, she said. Why not? I asked. It's so humiliating, she said. For you? I said, even though I knew that's what she meant. Yes, she said. To be deceived by someone you've trusted for forty years. He'll be back, I said. If he comes back, she said, he'll be a different person. And he'll come back to a different person. No, I said, but didn't get any further. Sonja was standing in the doorway. She cried out my name. I closed my eyes, I'd no strength left, I wanted to be taken care of. Mom! she cried. When I heard her standing right next to me, I opened my eyes and smiled at her, then closed them again. Mom explained what had happened. I didn't say anything, I wanted to be helpless, to be left in Sonja's hands. She brought cushions and put them under my shoulders and head, and I asked if I could get a pill. She was gone a while, it must have been then that she rang for an ambulance, but she didn't say anything about it when she came back out. She gave me the pill and asked how I was. Fine, I said, and even though it was true, I hadn't intended her to believe it. I did have an ache in my shoulder, but I was fine. She looked at me for quite a while, then she went up to the veranda and carried down the lounger. But not for me. For Mom. When I thought about it, it seemed only right, but at the same time she could have asked, if only to have allowed me the opportunity to give it up. Mom protested, she wanted me to have it. No, said Sonja, you sit down there. I didn't say anything. I thought: I told Sonja I was fine, that's the reason. Sonja helped Mom onto the lounger, then went into the house. The lawn felt hard beneath me, I wondered how long Sonja was planning to leave me there, after all I didn't know she'd rang the hospital. It was completely quiet, and I heard a car pull in front of the house and the doorbell ring. After a while, Sonja and two men in white came out onto the veranda and down the steps. They went straight to Mom. One of them spoke with her, the other one turned to me and stared at my leg. How long have you had that? he asked, pointing at the cast. A week, I said. Did you fall off the roof? he asked. Car crash, I said. I turned my face away. Is this really necessary, said Mom. Yes, Mom, said Sonja. The one who had spoken to me went to fetch a stretcher, the other one came over and asked how I was. Good, I said. Sonja must have told him about my shoulder, because he leaned over me and examined it. His assistant came with the stretcher, and they lifted me onto it. They carried me up the steps and into the bedroom. Sonja walked in front to show them the way. They lay me down on the bed, then left, Sonja too. She returned shortly afterwards. I'm going along to the hospital with Mom, she said. Okay, I said. Do you need anything? she asked. No, I said. She left. I hadn't meant to be so short, not really, after all I realized Mom might also need her help.

After a while it was completely quiet in the house. My eyes slowly closed, and I saw that great deserted landscape, that's painful to see, it's far too big, and far too desolate, and in a way it's both within me and around me. I opened my eyes to make it go away, but I was so tired, they closed by themselves. Probably due to the pills. I'm not afraid, I said out loud, just to say something. I said it a few times. Then I don't remember any more.

I awoke in the half-light. The curtains were drawn, the alarm clock showed four-thirty. The bedroom door was ajar, and a thin strip of light fell in through the gap. There was a bottle of water on the nightstand, and the bedpan was within easy reach of my good hand. I had no excuse to wake Sonja. I switched on the light and began to read *Maigret and the Dead Girl*, which Sonja had had with her. After a while I noticed I was hungry, but it was too early to call Sonja. I continued reading. When the clock showed six-thirty I began to grow impatient and slightly irritated. I thought it very inconsiderate of Sonja not to have left some sandwiches for me, she should have realized I'd wake up during the night. I lay there listening for any sounds in the house, but it was utterly silent. I pictured Sonja, and a different appetite took hold. I saw her more clearly than I had ever seen her in reality, and I didn't do anything to erase the image. I lay like that for a long time, until I heard an alarm clock ring. I picked up the book, but didn't read it. I waited. Eventually I called out for her. Then she came. She was wearing a pink bathrobe. I lay with the book in my hand so she'd see I had been awake. I heard the alarm clock, I said. You were fast asleep, she said, I didn't want to wake you. Are you in any pain? My shoulder hurts, I said. Will I get you a pill? she said. Yes, please, I said. She left. She was barefoot. Her heels didn't touch the ground. I placed the book on the nightstand. She returned with the pill and a glass of water. She held me behind the shoulder. I could see one of her breasts. Then I asked her to put another pillow behind me. You look so pretty, I said. Are you more comfortable now? she asked. Yes, thanks, I said. I'll make you breakfast soon, she said, I just need to get dressed. That's not necessary, I said. Aren't you hungry? she said. Oh yes, I said. She looked at me. I wasn't able to interpret her look. Then she left. She was gone a long time.

When she brought me breakfast, she was dressed. She was wearing a loose-fitting blouse buttoned right up. She said I should try to sit up, and she fetched some cushions, which she put behind my back. She was different. She looked everywhere but at me. She placed the tray with sandwiches and coffee on the duvet in front of me. Shout if you need anything, she said, and left.

After I'd eaten, I made up my mind not to call her, she could come of her own accord. I put the cup and plate on the nightstand and let the tray drop onto the floor, I was pretty sure she'd hear it. I lay waiting, for a long time, but she didn't come. I thought about how I'd forgotten to ask her how Mom was. Then I thought about how, when I was better, I'd be all on my own. I'd have the house all to myself, there would be no one who'd know when I was coming and going, and no one would know what I was up to. I wouldn't need to hide.

At last she came. I'd been feeling the effects of the pill for quite some time, and I was considerably better disposed towards her. I asked how Mom was doing, and she said that she was just getting up. I thought she was in hospital, I said. No, she said, it was only cuts and bruises. I told her what Mom had said to me about Dad. At first she looked like she didn't believe me, then it was like her whole body froze, her gaze too, and she said: That's . . . that's . . . disgusting! I was taken aback by her vehement reaction, after all she was a modern young woman. These things happen, I said. She stared at me as if I'd said something wrong. Oh, sure, yeah, she said, then picked the tray up off the floor and planted the cup and plate hard down on it. Don't let Mom know I told you, I said. Why not? she said. She asked me not to, I said. So why did you then? she said. I thought you should know, I said. Why? she said. I didn't reply, I was beginning to grow quite irritated, I certainly didn't like being told off. So the two of us would have a little secret? she said, in a tone I wasn't supposed to like. Yes, why not, I said. She looked at me, for quite a while, then she said: I think we both have different ideas about each other. That's a pity, I said. I closed my eyes. I heard her leave and close the door behind her. It hadn't been closed since I had come home from the hospital, and she knew I wanted it open. I was already angry, and that closed door didn't serve to lessen my anger. I wanted her out of the house, I didn't want to see her anymore. I wasn't so helpless that I needed to put up with all this. I hadn't done her any harm.

It took quite some time before I calmed down again. Then I thought about how the way she had behaved probably had more to do with Dad than with me, and once she had a chance to think it over, she'd see how unreasonable she had been.

But I couldn't quite manage to relax, and I had to admit to myself that I was dreading her return. I kept thinking I heard footsteps outside the door, and I'd close my eyes and pretend to be asleep. And I was just as relieved each time when she didn't come. Finally I lay there with my eyes closed just listening and waiting, and then I don't remember anymore until I saw Mom at the end of the bed, standing looking at me, a gauze dressing on her forehead, and a kind of bonnet on her head. Were you having a bad dream? she said. Was I talking in my sleep? I said. No, she said, but you were making faces. Are you in pain? Yes, I said. I'll go get you a pill, she said. She could hardly walk. I thought Sonja was probably embarrassed about having behaved in such an unreasonable manner, and that was why Mom had come instead of her, but when Mom came back with the pill, she said: Well, it's just the two of us now. She said it as if I was already aware of it. I didn't reply. She gave me the pill and offered to hold me up behind the shoulder, but I told her it wasn't necessary. I put the pill in my mouth and drank from the bottle. She sat down on the chair by the window. She said: Sonja was worried it would be too much for me, but she really wanted to get back. I nodded. Yes, she said, she said that you understood why she had to leave. Yes, I said. She smiled at me, then she said: You don't know how grateful I am. For what? I said, even though I knew what she meant. When I came around and saw you lying there beside me, she said, and I thought, at least William cares about me. Of course I do, I said. I closed my eyes. After a while I heard her get up and leave. I opened my eyes and thought: if she only knew.

Everything Like Before

The fat waiter was standing well in under the battered old corrugated-iron roof, smoking. It was a little after three o'clock, and the thermometer over his shoulder showed thirty-nine degrees. He tossed the butt away and went into the dim bar where the little Scot was sitting, playing solitaire.

Carl turned and saw a small fishing boat round the long, narrow breakwater. Just beyond, the sea disappeared in a haze of heat.

He sipped his beer, it had become tepid. The fishing boat vanished and everything was motionless.

But only for a moment. Zakarias's little green Hilux appeared by the corner of the train station. It pulled over and parked beneath the dappled shade of the tousled palm tree. Zakarias got out and began lifting cases of wine and Coke out of the back. The fat waiter came out of the bar and called out something Carl didn't understand. Zakarias answered. The waiter worked his fat thighs past one another and walked over to the truck. They began to carry the cases into the bar.

On his way back to pick up more, Zakarias looked over at Carl and called out:

—Hallo. Your wife not here?

—No. She is sick.

He patted his stomach to illustrate his lie.

—Sorry. Good wife—okay?

—Okay.

They carried in the rest of the cases. Then it was quiet again.

Carl finished his beer, left some coins on the table and stood up. He walked into the alley by the coopers. The shadow from the southwest-facing row of houses wasn't enough to cover him: the sun burned mercilessly.

He climbed the dark staircase of the guesthouse, up to the third floor. The door of the room was locked. He knocked, but Nina didn't answer. He called her name. Nothing. He had been so sure she was inside that he hadn't looked to see if the key was hanging in the reception. He went down to get it. It wasn't there.

Damn her, he thought, and went out into the harsh light. He walked back the same way. The table hadn't been cleared, the coins were still there. He sat down, facing the dark doorway. He put the coins in his pocket. The fat waiter didn't appear, and after a while Carl got up and went into the bar where the large ceiling fan made for a hint of a cooler atmosphere. The cook and the Scot were playing chess. Carl asked for a beer. Then he sat down at another table, further in, under the corrugated-iron roof where the light wasn't as strong. He was surprised that Nina could be capable of pretending she wasn't in the room, it wasn't like her—and in a flash of awareness he realized: I don't know her.

He drank. He thought: I'm going to stay here, she knows where to find me. I'm going to get drunk, slowly drunk.

He drank himself into a state of resentment before reaching a state of indifference, but without getting particularly drunk. People began arriving, and at four-thirty the waiter put on the record player, the siesta was over. The little Scot came out of the bar and sat down at the table closest to the door.

Carl drank, slowly, but willfully.

It was his turn today.

It had been Nina's yesterday.

It had started so well. They had been sitting at "Barbarossa" over some fish and a bottle of white wine. The brief twilight came and went, and the soft darkness fell. They talked about how the light seemed to slip out of the narrow streets and gather over the sea before disappearing over the horizon. They drank wine, touched hands, and things were good. The darkness around them grew, they paid and walked towards the old square, hand in hand.

They found a small table outside a café and ordered beer. Nina wanted a raki afterwards, and then one more. Everything was good; Carl had a real feeling of intimacy. Then Nina suggested they move on. They strolled through narrow, dimly lit streets, heading nowhere in particular.

They suddenly heard bouzouki music. They followed the sound, and it led them to a small taverna. The man playing was in his late fifties. They sat down at the only unoccupied table and ordered raki. There were photographs and newspaper pictures of the man playing hanging up behind the bar. "He must be well known," said Nina, buoyed. She drained her glass of raki and signaled to the skinny old woman behind the bar for another. Carl passed. And all of a sudden Nina wasn't with him any longer. She was sitting looking around the premises; she had got that peculiar, direct look in her eye—desirous, and at the same time, innocent. She zeroed on three men at a table by the door, either all three or one of them, he didn't know. What he did know was that he had to alter, or if necessary spoil her mood, or else things would turn out badly. But he couldn't do anything, not right away. When she wanted yet another raki, he asked with a smile—albeit a rather anxious smile—if she intended on getting drunk. "I'm fine," she replied, beaming at the musician and the three men by the door. Shortly after, the old woman behind the bar came over and filled up their glasses, probably at the request of one of the three. Carl said she didn't actually have to drink it, but she did. He followed suit; he had lost. Whatever happens, happens, he thought, it's what she wants after all, it's like she has this urge within her. Nevertheless, shortly afterwards he said he wanted to go. "Are you cross?" she asked, and he denied it, because it didn't cover it, he was sad, and perplexed, and perhaps a little riled. Yes, ever so slightly riled. He was an abandoned husband right in front of his own wife—damn right he was upset. He motioned to the landlady, smiled and paid, smiled at Nina as well, and at the musician, nobody would be able to tell anything by the look on his face, everything was normal, everything was good. He stood up and asked if she was coming. "Just as we were starting to enjoy ourselves," she said. "We?" he said, and smiled.

She went with him.

Neither of them spoke. She walked a few paces behind.

They came down to the harbor, and Nina said: "You're not planning on going home, are you?" He equivocated. "I'm not planning on going home," she said. "Only if you don't drink more raki," he said. "Christ, how very kind of you," she said. "Yes," he said. "A beer then," she said.

She picked a table, at the place with the biggest crowd. Carl tried to think of something to say, something to bring her back, but couldn't. In order to escape the uncomfortable silence, he went to the toilet, and he took his time. When he returned, she had begun talking to two Greeks at the next table; they were speaking in English, asking about Nina—where she was from, where she lived, how long she was staying. They were friendly, not flirtatious, and polite. Carl liked them, particularly the one sitting closest to Nina, who spoke the best English, was called Nikos, and was here on holiday from Athens. After a while, Nina moved her chair nearer Nikos, and Carl, smiling between gritted teeth, said in Norwegian: "You don't need to take a bite out of him." She looked at him. "You have to speak English," she said.

After that he had nothing more to say. Everything took its course. Nina ordered, inadvertently as it were, more beer. Nikos's friend left. Nikos pulled his chair over to their table, Nina placed her hand, inadvertently as it were, on his bare arm. Carl pretended not to notice, or rather: as if it didn't mean anything, and carried on the conversation about the trials after the fall of the junta, trials which in Nikos's opinion had been a farce and a disaster. Nina interrupted and asked if he was a lawyer. Nikos laughed, placed his free hand upon hers—but only for a second—and said he worked for an insurance company. Nina said she wouldn't have thought that to look at him. Carl checked his watch and said it was getting late. Nikos checked his watch as well, and agreed. He said he was going the same way. They paid. Nina suggested they walk along the beach. Carl and Nikos walked on either side of her. Carl saw Nina taking Nikos by the hand, it pained him. He moved a little away from them, not much, but enough for the small waves on the beach to prevent him from hearing what they were saying. Nina halted abruptly, turned towards Nikos and kissed him on the mouth. It wasn't a prolonged kiss, and Nikos was merely passive. But he didn't let go of her hand. Carl didn't say anything, just stood there looking at them. It was he who had the faint light in his face, theirs lay in darkness. He stood looking at them silhouetted in the lights from the boardwalk, and he saw Nikos withdraw his hand. Then they walked on, nobody spoke. Carl walked a few meters ahead, wouldn't turn around, he had some pride. He went diagonally across towards the lights, heard them following behind. They reached the road, Carl continued on in the direction of the guesthouse, Nina and Nikos chatting behind him, Nina laughed. Then he turned after all and saw they were holding hands. They were almost at the guesthouse. It's over now, thought Carl, don't crawl, it's over now anyway. He quickened his pace. Nina called out something or other, but he pretended not to hear. He entered the guesthouse, nodded to Manos, who was half-asleep beside a small TV, and got the key behind the counter. He hurried up to the room. The balcony door was open, allowing some streetlight to fall into the room. He didn't switch on the lights, but went straight out onto the balcony, which was almost directly above the entrance. He couldn't hear anything. He leaned over the railing and looked down. They weren't there. He sat down, lit up a cigarette. After a while he heard the door being opened, he sat motionless, thought for one desperate moment that she was not alone. She was. She stood beside him. "What's wrong with you?" she said. He didn't reply. "You're always doing this," she said. He held his tongue and he didn't give her an answer, because that was what she was after. "Damn it," she said and went into the room. He tossed the half-finished cigarette down on the street and lit up another. She turned on the light. "Have I done something wrong?" she asked. He didn't reply. She came back out. "Are you not going to bed?" "Not yet," he replied. "Are you going to punish me now?" she asked. "For what?" he replied, thinking it a good answer.

"For not being able to satisfy me with that quick dick of yours." She went back in, turned out the light. He sat there, his heart wouldn't slow, his blood pounded and pounded. Now it's over, he thought, it's got to be over sometime.

He smoked three more cigarettes and presumed she'd fallen asleep. He went quietly in, got undressed, drew the portières, groped his way to the bed, and pulled the sheet over him. Nina moved. "Is it something I've done?" she asked. He didn't reply. "Christ, you're such a sadist," she said. He lay for a while, trying to think up the worst thing he could say, and then he said it: "You told me once about a friend of yours who was in the habit of flaunting her cunt. When I looked at you tonight, it occurred to me what you meant. You should . . ."

Suddenly she was on top of him, he was caught completely off guard, he felt her fingers close around his throat and heard her hiss: "I'll kill you." Her grip on his throat wasn't firm, but he panicked and hit out. She loosened her grip, but didn't stop fighting. He pushed her away, got out from under the sheet and stood on the floor. She lay there gasping for breath. He drew the portière aside and went onto the balcony, before coming back in again to get his clothes and cigarettes. It was one-thirty._

At two-fifteen he went in and got into bed. Nina was asleep. At nine-thirty he awoke and got quietly up out of bed. Nina was asleep. She had kicked the sheet off. She had a bruise, the size of a fist, on the front of her left shoulder. For a moment he was almost overcome by a sudden tenderness, but then he remembered. He closed the door quietly behind him.

The fat waiter met his gaze. Carl pointed at the empty glass. The waiter nodded and went into the bar. Carl missed Nina—and hoped she wouldn't come.

Just then she arrived. She was wearing a blue blouse that covered her shoulder.

—There you are, she said and sat down.

She smiled slightly. He didn't smile, avoided meeting her eyes.

As if I'm the one who should have a guilty conscience, he thought.

—I must have been drunk, she said.—Did I go for you?

He nodded.

—Why?

—I told you what I thought of you.

—Oh. Right.

The waiter came with a bottle of beer. Nina ordered one too.

—Right, said Carl.

—And what was it you thought of me?

—That I suddenly realized what you'd meant when you once told me about a girl who flaunted her cunt.

—Oh. Why was that?

—You don't remember any more than you want to, do you?

—I remember getting angry and going for you.

—And Nikos?

—Nikos?

He related the details which had been the most humiliating, apart from what she had said about him being unable to satisfy her. He was quite thorough and expected her to be devastated.

The waiter brought her beer just as he was finished saying his piece. She poured it into the glass, slowly, then took a long mouthful, before she said:

—Jesus, Carl. That's nothing to be getting worked up about, I was drunk. And after all, I didn't do anything wrong.

—Right, right. Okay, sure.

—Carl.

—We don't understand one another. What would you say if I'd done what you did?

—But you're not like that.

—Oh, Jesus.

—But it's important. You're you and I'm me. You don't know me.

—No.

—Don't mock me.

He looked away from her, stared into space and said:

—Just now, before you came, I was sitting here missing you, but at the same time I was hoping you wouldn't come. I felt a sort of anxiety about you suddenly turning up. As if I ought to have a guilty conscience or even had reason to have one. I've experienced it before. Longing for you but not wanting you to come—it's schizophrenic. Last night I decided it has to come to an end. I'm sick and tired of being trampled on.

—But I was drunk.

—You wanted to get drunk, just like all the other times. And when you're drunk, you invariably walk all over me. I'm not so stupid that I don't realize it's due to something, something in our relationship, something you ought to take the consequences of, but you don't. You suppress it, get drunk, and walk all over me. I'm not a piece of shit, and I'm tired of being treated like one.

—But you never said anything, why didn't you say something?

—I can't stick my nose into your business like that, I just can't. I don't have any right to you—I only have the right to turn my back when someone toys with me and humiliates me. If I had said more than I did, then it would've just been even more humiliating. I should have left, but I was too pathetic to leave.

She didn't say anything. He had a sudden feeling of emptiness. He poured beer into the glass, even though it was almost full. He wanted to leave. He hoped she'd say something hurtful or aggressive to give him a reason to go. But she didn't say anything. They both sat on each side of the small table, Carl pretending as if he was looking at what was going on around them. Nina with her head slightly tilted and her eyes resting on the green tabletop. A couple of minutes passed. Carl got up and went into the toilet. He stood there, pissing, and was sad. He went back out into the dim bar but he stopped short when he heard jazz music coming from the record player behind the counter. A saxophone was coming over the speakers, singing of a tenderness he was in need of. He asked for a raki so that he wasn't just standing there. He could see Nina, he listened to the music and looked at her. He thought: why do I have a guilty conscience?

He drained the glass, went outside, sat down, and said:

—I have a guilty conscience, it's ludicrous, but also slightly sad. It may well not be through any fault of yours, it could be due to a lack of self-esteem on my part.

It wasn't entirely clear to him why he had said it and what he wanted her to say in reply, but she didn't answer at all, just sat there looking straight ahead. And all at once her complaint from the night before, which hadn't been referred to, planted itself between them, like a fence and like freedom, and as he stood up he said:

—I'm going home.

He placed a banknote on the table and left. She said something behind him, but he didn't catch it. He didn't know where he was going. He walked towards the town, into the cluster of narrow streets and lanes. The sun was low, only peeping out between the rows of houses now and then.

He had left her, but she remained stuck on his mind.

When he didn't know where he had got to, he sat down at a table and drank raki, ate snails and berated himself harshly. Slave, damned slave soul, every time you try to exact some justice for yourself, you collapse with compassion for your tormentor!

He drank, and it grew dark, and he got on well with himself. He went from place to place and got drunk. He grinned when he noticed he no longer said "you" but "we" when he talked to himself. "We'll stay out all night, will we?" he said. We'll get drunk and sleep on the beach, then she'll have something to wonder about. To hell with her. We'll sleep right where she stood and kissed that damned insurance man. But first we'll get drunk.

And he did.

His memory of the rest of the night was hazy. He vaguely remembered Nina turning up—he didn't know where—and that he refused to go home with her, he was headed for the beach. When he got there he threw up, and it was degrading, he remembered that.

He woke up before noon, at the guesthouse. Nina ran her hand across his chest and through his hair and told him she understood.

He knew she didn't.

But maybe she understood a little.

Her fingers stroked and caressed, pushing more and more of the sheet away from his body. He remembered and wanted to resist, otherwise what was done would become undone. But his desire pressed on, and she saw it and took matters in hand, and there was no way out.

Just before he came, she issued an inarticulate cry, and a prolonged trembling passed through her body. He didn't know what to believe, but he knew what she wanted him to believe.

He felt sad and empty.

She lay twirling his hair around her finger.

—Now everything's like before, isn't it? she said.

He thought about it.

—Yes, it is, he said.

Norwegian Literature Series

The Norwegian Literature Series was initiated by the Royal Norwegian Consulate Generals of New York and San Francisco, and the Royal Norwegian Embassy in Washington, D.C., together with NORLA (Norwegian Literature Abroad). Evolving from the relationship begun in 2006 with the publication of Jon Fosse's *Melancholy*, and continued with Stig Sæterbakken's *Siamese* in 2010, this multi-year collaboration with Dalkey Archive Press will enable the publication of major works of Norwegian literature in English translation.

Drawing upon Norway's rich literary tradition, which includes such influential figures as Knut Hamsun and Henrik Ibsen, the Norwegian Literature Series will feature major works from the late modernist period to the present day, from revered figures like Tor Ulven to first novelists like Kjersti A. Skomsvold.